ZRJC
8/13

Wrestling with Tom Sawyer

Other Books in the Enchanted Attic Series

BOOK FOUR

Wrestling with Tom Sawyer

L.L. SAMSON

ZONDER**kidz**

ZONDERVAN.com/
AUTHORTRACKER
follow your favorite authors

ZONDERKIDZ

Wrestling with Tom Sawyer
Copyright © 2013 by L. L. Samson

This title is also available as a Zondervan ebook.
Visit www.zondervan.com/ebooks

Requests for information should be addressed to:

Zonderkidz, 5300 Patterson Ave., S.E., Grand Rapids, Michigan 49530

Library of Congress Cataloging-in-Publication Data

Samson, L. L., 1964-
    Wrestling with Tom Sawyer / L.L. Samson.
        pages cm. — (Enchanted attic series ; book 4)
        Summary: When twins Linus and Ophelia and their friend, Walter, bring Tom
    Sawyer into the real world, Tom immediately starts trouble but when Ophelia, with
    whom he has fallen in love, is kidnapped, Tom is determined to save her.
        ISBN 978-0-310-74057-5 (softcover)
        [1. Space and time—Fiction. 2. Characters in literature—Fiction. 3. Twain,
    Mark, 1835-1910. Adventures of Tom Sawyer—Fiction. 4. Kidnapping—Fiction. 5.
    Books and reading--Fiction. 6. Brothers and sisters--Fiction. 7. Twins—Fiction. 8.
    Orphans—Fiction.] I. Title.
        PZ7.S1696Wre 2013
        [Fic]—dc23   2013009465

Cover design: Kris Nelson
Interior design: Ben Fetterly
Interior Illustrations: Antonio Caparo

Printed in the United States of America

13 14 15 16 17 18 19 /DCI/ 22 21 20 19 18 17 16 15 14 13 12 11 10 9 8 7 6 5 4 3 2 1

For Isaac, with love,
because you love these books.

Contents

one

Some Things Remain Hidden in the Most Obscure Places for an Exceedingly Long Time; Hopefully You Are Not One of Them

or Let Us Drop You into the Story Right Away, Shall We?

*L*inus Easterday, his twin sister Ophelia, and their best friend Walter were as electrified as you would be at the discovery of a secret tunnel in the basement of your school.

It started out as a seemingly regular day. Walter had been savoring his lunch (chicken, noodles, and fresh broccoli beneath a flaky casserole crust), silently thanking God that the school cook was back on duty. Her multipierced appearance may be more suited to life in a traveling circus, but her cooking was utterly heavenly compared to Madrigal Pierce's compulsory concoction (mixture, medley, blend) of canned-food meals.

Yet even the ghastly victuals (dreadful food) were worth the freedoms that summer afforded Walter. And to think, barely four months ago Walter called London home. Now he was venturing to the park at whim, tramping the streets of Kingscross with his friends, and sometimes just lazing on the banks of the Bard River at three in the blazing afternoon, all proving that he had successfully adapted to life in the States. Amazing how quickly a lad can refashion his life, is it not? And Walter needed serious alterations.

Madrigal Pierce (headmistress, chief fundraiser, algebra teacher, and dean of student life at The Pierce School for Young People) stepped up to the microphone at the far end of the students' dining hall as if she owned the place, which she did—and still does. *(Thank goodness, especially after the schemes of that wily* (smart in a sneaky way) *brother of hers.)*

She cinched her customary shawl around her shoulders and elevated an index card. The distance from her hand to her face proclaimed a need for reading glasses that she obstinately refused to purchase. "Attention pupils!" she began in her forthright voice. "As promised, notes that have been confiscated during class will be read before the entire school during the lunch hour."

She extracted a folded piece of paper from the pocket of her voluminous brown skirt. (*Voluminous*, in this case, means the designer employed several yards of fabric which ended up on Madrigal's slight frame.)

"This particular communiqué is from Miss Jane Meyers to Mister Jordon Van Meter," Madrigal said. Then clearing her throat, she read,

"Jane: Someone said you sound like an owl.

"Jordon: Who?"

After a momentary silence in which the students looked at one another questioningly, the lunchroom exploded with riotous laughter. The left corner of Madrigal's habitually pinched lips lifted. Then Ms. Pierce crumpled the piece of notebook paper into a ball and lobbed it over her shoulder. "That's enough of that, then."

Walter, his brown eyes as round as the aforementioned owl's, looked at Linus and Ophelia as if to say, "Who is this woman and what happened to our headmistress?"

Ms. Pierce cleared her throat once more and patted the side of her almost black hair, which was scraped back into a ruthless chignon (bun). "Rumors have been flying around the school about the renovations in the northeast corner of our fair institution." The crisp edge to her voice had returned, like a fringe of frost around a curled brown leaf.

Ahh, thought Walter, *there's our Madge*.

"These rumors include the discovery of a tunnel hitherto unknown by the faculty and staff. I assure you that while the tunnel is indeed factual, tales of skeletons, buried treasure, a Native American graveyard, and an Olympic-sized swimming pool are utterly fictitious."

Drat, thought Ophelia. She had been hoping that the rumor about the pool was not a rumor at all. Imagine it! The hidden pool would be like something out of Rome with pillars all around, Greek statuary, and fountains spouting at both ends. And it would be heated, of course.

"Furthermore," Ms. Pierce continued, "we've clearly cordoned off the construction zone. Anyone and everyone found inside the confines of the work area will not only lose their town privileges, but will also be assigned punitive work duty."

In other words, no leaving school after 9 P.M. sharp, because you can bet your sweet Aunt Ida's alligator purse that you will be scrubbing the blackened bottoms of pots and pans from after supper until the quiet hours of the late evening for at least a week. When not in class, the students must be in their rooms or the dorm lounges studying or reading quietly. (Or, truth be told, texting each other from across the room.)

The Pierce School for Young People is primarily a boarding school for children of either the once well-heeled (wealthy) who'd fallen on harder times, or for those who had recently accumulated their wealth and were snubbed by the well-heeled. The mixture of "old money" and "new money" worked well enough, but only because Ms. Pierce herself allowed for nothing else. Give people a common adversary, and it's amazing what they'll forget about!

As the students left the dining hall for their fourth-hour classes, Walter pulled Linus and Ophelia aside. "Eleven-thirty at the tunnel entrance?" he asked.

"Yep," said Linus, pulling off his school tie (this was allowed after lunch).

"Do you have torches?" Walter asked, tucking his button-down shirt into his khaki pants and straightening the navy-and-orange striped tie underneath his collar. *Though a reformed street rat, the lad knows how to make a proper appearance. And a hearty "Bravo!" to that, I might add.* Walter reached into his blazer pocket for his comb.

"No, but we have flashlights," Ophelia offered. Her uniform had the same crisp classiness as Walter's, except with a skirt beneath the blue blazer.

Walter tried not to roll his eyes. In London "torch" is the name used for a flashlight. But never mind, really. No need to offend Ophelia who, in his estimation, was turning into a real looker. Her sable (dark brown) hair shone like glass and matched her eyes. You had to admire a girl with such natural color coordination.

Linus, Ophelia, and Walter had survived several adventures together over the summer. And Walter, of all people, knew that a smart girl like Ophelia was a find.

One must give Walter credit for recognizing a good thing. Most of the male students at Kingscross University, where I work in the English Department, gravitate toward the girls who spend more time in the tanning booth than in the library and who would be better suited for a reality television horror show than the halls of learning.

Oh my, yes. The future would promise to be quite bleak if not for young people like these three and, hopefully, you as well.

Ophelia heaved her satchel onto the midnight blue sofa in the not-so-secret attic that the twins found shortly after they moved in with their Aunt Portia and Uncle Augustus, also twins. Their parents, the Doctors Easterday (PhD, naturally), had dumped Linus and Ophelia there at the beginning of the summer, so they could sail off for five years to study butterflies on the Island of Willis (discovered by Willis Cranston of Hohokus, New Jersey, while parasailing).

Granted, previously undiscovered species of these winged wonders were in residence on Stu. But to desert their own offspring, leaving them to navigate the teenage years without their parents? Hardly coincidental and atrocious to boot!

Some readers want everyone in books such as this to be good people, for the children therein to grow up in a home with two parents who love each other and are on constant lookout for the best interests of their children. While I'm sure those families exist, and hopefully you belong to one of them, if I portrayed the Drs. Easterday as model parents, it would be an unmitigated falsehood (a pure lie). In these stories, they are examples of what not to do concerning one's offspring.

A letter had arrived from the maternal Dr. Easterday, and Ophelia threw it on top of her book bag. "I can already tell you what it says," she said to Linus, who sat on a stool in front of his lab table watching a beaker full of purple ooze bubbling like a tar pit over a low flame.

Linus knew what it said, too. Butterflies this. Butterflies that. Butterflies here, there, and everywhere. And make sure you earn straight As, take your vitamins every morning, and limit your computer time.

And just how are you doing, Linus and Ophelia?

Oh, silly me. Those words were much like planes disappearing in the Bermuda Triangle, never to be found.

"Two more days," Linus said, pointing to a white circle painted on the worn wooden planks of the attic floor. It was September the ninth.

On 11:11 P.M. of September the eleventh, sparks would fly.

"I can't wait," said Ophelia.

Some people are gluttons for punishment.

A glutton for punishment is someone who knowingly advances into difficult situations. Which is fine if they accept their decision as their own, but it's unacceptable if they come crying to you expecting sympathy afterward. Don't give it to them, or you'll be listening to their whining for the rest of your life. Who wants that!

While awaiting the arrival of the infamous date and time, the trio of friends found other ways to occupy themselves. In fact, they had become accustomed to clandestine activity (sneaking around). Now concealed in dark pants, dark shirts, and dark hoodies, the gang traversed (crossed) the barricade that snaked around the perimeter of the construction zone on the first floor of The Pierce School.

Madrigal's no-good, terrible, and very bad brother Johann had set a fire in August that had destroyed the formal parlor of the mansion (owned and occupied by the Pierce family for more than two centuries), which now served as the school.

The construction crew had dismantled the charred floor, exposing the basement underneath. The windows still waited for glass panes, and the once blood-red walls were mostly black with soot. Like the workers, the three friends now entered the parlor from the veranda in the garden outside, hoping to keep all noises from echoing around the grand marble entry hall on the other side of the room.

Without a word, Ophelia distributed the flashlights. Linus procured (got) an aluminum ladder from the supplies the work crew left at the school, and he lowered it against the basement wall. "After you," he whispered to the others.

They soon stood in the basement facing the arched opening of the tunnel.

Walter released a sigh of relief. "Nobody should hear us now."

"True," whispered Linus, wondering who would lead the way down the dark passage. At least they would get away from the lingering, nostril-coating smell of the fire.

"I'll go first," said Ophelia, reading her brother's mind. Linus hated talking more than he hated doing laundry. *(Exhibit one: the pyramid of dirty clothes in his bedroom is almost a wonder of the modern world.)* So the phenomenon of his sister's ability to pick up on his thoughts—he dubbed them "transmissions"—was a gift of twinhood for which Linus always felt grateful.

Ophelia thumbed on her flashlight as the boys did the

same. She shone its beam down the subterranean (underground) corridor. Stone walls and a dirt floor lit up beneath the searching eye of the light.

She shrugged. "Hmm." Then stepped forward without hesitation.

What a woman! thought Walter.

The tunnel wasn't high enough for Linus's six-foot-two-inch frame to walk through without bending his neck a bit. And the narrow width of the tunnel allowed for only one person to walk through comfortably, but Linus stayed close behind his sister quite easily.

Serving as the caboose of their three-car train of explorers, Walter, feeling not so far removed from the mean streets of his old neighborhood, allowed his survival instincts to kick in front and center. So far so good.

It was a bit disappointing, actually. Two weeks before, Walter had started taking classes at Mr. Yang's Most Excellent School of Kung Fu. Now he wanted to try out his new moves on the bullies who frequented Paris Park across the street, but they hadn't even placed so much as a toe on the lush grass that spread like a green velvet mantle (covering) over the park's open spaces.

While Ophelia dreamed of finding a classical pool, Walter hoped to stumble across a more criminal element, such as smuggled treasure. Linus was just along for the fun.

It takes all kinds, I suppose.

"Wow," Ophelia said when they were about fifty yards in, and then she suddenly stopped walking.

Linus, a genius of mind but not of body, ran into her back. "Sorry."

"What is it, O. J.?" asked Walter, employing the new

nickname he'd given Ophelia. He is what some people might call a physical genius, picking up sports with little to no effort and always knowing where to be and what to do in a fight.

Disclaimer: The management in no way condones the use of violence or force. Further questions? Call 1-555-888-1111 and press pound. Thank you.

"The floor," said Ophelia, "it's limestone now, and the walls seem to be carved out of limestone too."

"A probable cave system!" said Linus.

"I wonder where it leads?" she asked.

Now Walter's instincts took over. "Let me take the lead, Ophelia. A drop-off might occur at any second."

"All right," Ophelia agreed. If someone was going to get hurt, it might as well not be her.

Now, you might think this extremely callous (heartless) of Ophelia, but her bookworm tendencies eclipsed any interest in athletics, and she knew Walter was clearly more equipped to lead the group in a subterranean expedition. The guy had a great set of reflexes.

Walter slid sideways past the twins, brushing against Ophelia's side as he did so (and feeling not one bit sad about it).

As Walter now took the lead, the trio angled their beams of light up and down and side to side.

"Dry so far," Linus observed, after they'd wandered the singular path for another minute or two.

The beams illuminated the path's end at another, wider path. They could go right or left, and none of them knew which was the road less traveled.

"We'd better not venture on," Walter said. "We might get lost, and we don't have a way to mark our trail."

And that has made all the difference. At least just then. Though it wasn't a very big difference, really.

I merely wanted to use a literary allusion (a reference to a previous work) there. But I have no compulsion (strong impulse) to tell you what it is. Ask your language arts teacher. And if he or she cannot locate it, then your parents should write a letter to the administration, post haste!

If you recognized it, then pat yourself on the back and know that you aren't counted as one of the dullards endangering our civilization!

two

Books Gone Rogue or at the Very Least, Missing

or Setting Up the Basic Problem to Keep the Reader Turning Pages

*W*ell! *If you do not deem this chapter's title a dandy of a humdinger (first-rate statement of remarkable excellence), then I, Bartholomew Inkster, LF (literary fussbudget, self-taught) cannot help you. I'm so proud of it, I believe I should treat myself to a triple espresso with white mocha at the coffee bar on the hipster block of Kingscross. Then again, not desiring to mortgage my house in order to afford such an indulgence, I shall instead procure a cup of java from the department lounge. The professors hate it when I do that, due to the obvious fact that the janitor is more well-read than they are and possesses finer literary tastes (if some of today's assigned readings are any indication).*

If you do not like that, feel free to take it up with the university's administration. Thank you.

Aunt Portia, with a ruby tiara resting atop her frizzy, apricot-colored hair, set a sizeable red platter on the kitchen table. When she'd read someplace that the elements of a meal should all coordinate, it failed to occur to her that the flavors should harmonize. In other words, who wants a plate of sweet pickles, tapioca pudding, and red beans? Instead, she took "coordinate" to mean that foods must go together by category or color.

That evening's meal displayed its theme loudly: the color purple. She artfully arranged eggplant rounds fried crisp, blueberry pancakes, blackberries, and grape-flavored fruit leather to resemble a gathering of carnival rides. If it hadn't been for the obvious color theme and the rectangular fruit leather, one might have thought she'd chosen a theme of circles.

As the platter was passed from twin to twin to twin to twin, each selecting items from the dusky assortment, Aunt Portia reported on her day. "I don't know what happened, but four of my rarest first editions are nowhere to be found!"

The family lived on the second and third floors above Portia's bookstore on Rickshaw Street. Seven Hills Better Books (hardbacks only, collectible first editions, and antiquarian volumes) kept Aunt Portia busy. Internet marketing, a new LED sign, and a coffee machine were her latest attempts at attracting new business.

Naturally, Seven Hills is my favorite shop in Kingscross, despite the coffee and the mess those cups make.

"Did you misplace them?" asked Uncle Augustus, looking smart in a quilted smoking jacket in a glistening shade of garnet. (Garnet is a dark red semiprecious stone.)

"I haven't ruled that out. But I've looked everywhere I can think to look. Nobody has reshelved books but me, and I can't remember anybody looking at them recently."

And why would they? Who would want to pay that much for Victor Hugo when you can purchase an entire collection *of his works on the Internet for $19.99 plus tax and $3.99 for shipping? It doesn't smell like mildewed socks, either.*

Augustus cut a slice of eggplant with the side of his fork. "It's a mystery, then."

"Hopefully one that's soon solved." Aunt Portia plucked the yellow damask napkin from beside her plate and laid it on her lap.

Uncle Augustus swallowed his bite, sipped some water, and then said, "On a happier note, the party plans are coming along swimmingly." He turned to Linus and Ophelia. "I'm going to need you to tidy up the yard after school tomorrow, Linus. And Ophelia, all of the windows as well as the baseboards need to be cleaned."

The twins' groans had no effect on their uncle who believed that hard physical labor hurt no one. *In other words, Linus and Ophelia have chores just like you do.*

Augustus threw a soiree (pronounced swah-**rey**) on the eleventh day of every month. And the theme of this month's party was *Along the Mississippi River—A Night with Mark Twain.* Augustus, once a concert musician with the Boston Philharmonic, was readying himself to play the part of one of America's most memorable and much beloved man of letters, Mark Twain (born Samuel Clemens in 1835).

Ophelia had readied her Becky Thatcher costume, and Linus, going for comfort, had chosen to emulate (imitate) Huckleberry Finn. Walter found a suit from Uncle Augustus's extensive costume collection that made him look like a riverboat captain.

"Our costumes are all set," Ophelia informed her uncle. "We're using *The Adventures of Tom Sawyer* as inspiration."

"Thank you, my dear."

After the twins cleared the table and washed the dishes, they decided to spend their last hour of daylight at Paris Park. Walter planned to join them in the attic after lights out by using the secret passage between a cleaning supply closet in The Pierce School and the third-floor bathroom of Linus and Ophelia's home. Having been in the States for only a few days, Walter had discovered it when midnight boredom set him to poking around the school. He is the type of person, as the old saying goes, who doesn't let grass grow under his feet. In other words, he's most likely never muttered the words "I'm bored" without making plans to rectify the situation.

Linus joined his girlfriend, Clarice Yardly-Poutsmouth, on the tennis court. He wasn't a bit concerned that she would thrash him at her favorite game. Clarice was the only student at The Pierce School whose family was old and yet still had heaps of money (although she wasn't all that impressed by it).

Ophelia read her paperback copy of *The Adventures of Tom Sawyer* while sitting on a bench near the Bard River that flowed beside the park and ran parallel with Rickshaw Street. She had almost finished the book—laughing at Tom's brash, boyish antics, admiring his pluck, and appreciating his sheer good luck—when a movement from further down the walking path beside the river caught her eye.

"Kyle!" She waved to the boy she'd met earlier that summer at the camp just upriver. The Bard River Camp for Kids gave children with special needs a fantastic summer to remember.

The outgoing lad waved back with his left hand, while his right piloted the joystick that steered his wheelchair— or what he likes to call his "spiffy black set of wheels." He zoomed up the path, halting next to her on the bench. "Hi, Ophelia!"

"How do you like The Pierce School so far?" she asked.

It was Kyle's first year at the school. The gang had been delighted when they'd seen the sixth grader at orientation. Though a tad young for a sixth grader, his math skills had earned him a scholarship from a foundation that paid for an exceptional education for physically challenged children like Kyle.

His blue eyes dropped, revealing a crescent of blond lashes. "Okay, I guess."

"What's wrong?"

"I don't know. I guess I don't like being the littlest kid there. And then there's this thing." He bumped the arm of the wheelchair with his hand.

Ophelia's heart twisted. "It's been only a week, bud. These things take time even for us older kids. You know that boy Lassiter Plum? I've never done one thing to him, and yet he snickers at me every time I walk by."

"I don't like him."

"Me either. But the point is, there will always be people like Lassiter Plum wherever we go. And you know what? We should feel sorry for them! Imagine having a mean heart like that."

"I'd hate that."

She took his hand. "Exactly. Hey! My aunt and uncle are having a party tomorrow evening. Want to come help us set up?"

His eyes cleared. "Do I?" He pumped a fist in the air. "Definitely!"

Ophelia checked her watch. "Well, good. Ten minutes to quiet hours. Do you mind if I walk back with you?"

Once across the street, Kyle and Ophelia cut through the garden at the side of The Pierce School. They eyed the construction site as they walked past.

"Too bad there's no swimming pool down there," Kyle said.

"Exactly what I was thinking."

Perhaps you should try the local YMCA, Ophelia.

Linus sat at his lab table in the attic, pondering a worthy project topic for the upcoming school science fair. Plenty of inspiration was available. You see, the attic laboratory—the entire building, actually—once belonged to Cato Grubbs, mad scientist and general troublemaker at large (on the loose). Nobody realized the wonders lingering in the uppermost reaches of the house until Linus and Ophelia discovered the hidden room soon after they moved in.

The lab table and the dark blue sofa with gold fringe were the most formidable of all the furnishings. But don't assume that the other tables and shelves stacked with volumes written in German, Italian, and a mysterious language (using an alphabet Linus had never seen before) didn't possess a decrepit (in this case, old and mildly battered) grandeur all their own. These shelves and tables also held cans containing everyday items such as bolts, hairpins, and river stones; bottles filled with brightly colored liquids that caught the sunlight when it shone through the trefoil window under the eaves; jars of powders; and tins of organic items such as aardvark toenails and mud from the Rhine River.

Considering its wide variety of contents, the attic might have won the award for Most Interesting Place in Town—if there was such a thing, that is.

Linus pondered three jars labeled A, B, and C. *It must have taken the genius who thought up those names all of three seconds to do so.* He pulled down a binder of detailed notes from his experiments, then opened Cato Grubbs's journal, checked and double-checked a formula, and pursed his lips. Something wasn't quite right with his current experiment. And despite his extraordinary efforts *(you try staying up three days in a row and checking the barometric pressure every ten minutes)*, he kept hitting a wall.

The rainbow beaker, as Linus called it, held the key. He was sure of it. *(By the way, he called it the "rainbow beaker" because it was filled with a liquid that retained its composition according to the light spectrum—ROY G BIV, don't you know—no matter how one tipped it.)* He just couldn't find a way to use it to unlock the door to the secrets of the enchanted circle.

This problem, however, had nothing to do with his science project. As it turns out, he wouldn't need any chemistry lab equipment for that. A wind tunnel would have been helpful, though, as Linus had decided he would design an airplane that would revolutionize the aeronautics industry.

Or so he hoped. *Aim high, dream big, and live large, I always say!*

three

Party On, Auggie! Party On, Portia!

or Introducing Side Characters
You've Come to Know and Love

(or in the Case of Professor Birdwistell,
Wish You Hadn't Come to Know at All)

onda, part-time hair stylist, part-time caterer and coffee bar owner (her most recent venture), worked on the food preparation for Uncle Auggie's party. As it usually did, Ronda's presence brought anyone of the male gender who currently occupied the house on Rickshaw Street flocking to the kitchen. Even Kyle sat in rapt attention as the most beautiful woman on the planet rolled out pastry for homemade apple dumplings. *(If you go blabbing that I said such, you will be proclaimed a liar of the first degree—never mind the fact that it's written right here in black and white.)* And Father Lou (the motorcycle riding, ponytailed priest at All Souls Episcopal Church across the street) cored apples that he and Ronda had picked during their date the previous afternoon.

Uncle Augustus pretended to rummage through the junk drawer for a tape measure he didn't need. And Walter sliced a ham while stealing surreptitious (furtive, secretive, going for unseen, really) glances at Ronda. Linus sat at the kitchen table eating a PB&J while flipping through one of his favorite periodicals, *Glider Planes Today*. He liked the sound of her voice.

Ronda chattered with her customary conviviality (friendly manner). Unlike some women with such powerful pulchritude (beauty), she failed to realize the matchless magnitude of her consummate comeliness (complete beauty).

I just employed a device called alliteration. *Alliteration employs words that begin with the same letter or sound. Annoying, isn't it?*

"I heard Clark's Antiques was burgled the other night," Ronda said, swiping her forearm across her glistening forehead.

Father Lou's eyebrows arched. "Did you actually use the word 'burgle,' Ronda?"

She giggled. "I did!"

"I like it!" he said with a laugh.

Oh dear me. Somebody fetch me a sleeve of Saltines to stave off my sudden onset nausea. Burgle it if you must.

Ophelia was listening in while she ironed the linen napkins in the dining room. "What happened?" she asked.

"Jonas told me that when he went to open the shop, the back door was ajar." (Slightly open.)

Clark's Antiques sits two doors down from Ronda's beauty salon and four doors down from Seven Hills bookshop, right next to Professor Birdwistell's house.

"Were the thieves still about?" asked Walter.

"Thankfully, no. But a French sideboard from the 1700s and two figurines were taken. And, if you can believe this, a brooch belonging to Marie Antoinette."

Ophelia set down the iron and rushed into the kitchen. "*The* Marie Antoinette?"

"None other." Ronda began filling the cored Pink Lady apples with a mixture of cinnamon, nutmeg, and brown sugar. *Beautiful and a wonderful cook, too. Father Lou's no dummy, as they say.*

Linus met Ophelia's glance. Could Cato Grubbs be broadening the scope of his thievery? You see, the mad scientist who founded the lab in the attic, was, to use a time-honored saying, a man with sticky fingers. They were even stickier, in fact, than Ronda's fingers were now as she sprinkled coarse sugar over the pastry.

"It's getting to be a problem." Father Lou finished stuffing the last apple. "Three people from our congregation have had valuable antiques taken from their homes."

Linus wondered if a similar thread ran through the fabric of all the crimes.

"Is there any connection between them?" asked Ophelia. "Other than antiques?"

"I don't know. But that's something to consider," said Father Lou. "Good thinking, Ophelia."

Linus frowned. She had gotten the thought from him, right?

Kyle finished slicing the block of Swiss cheese Ronda had given to him. "What else can I do?"

Ronda took a block of Muenster cheese out of the refrigerator. "How about more slicing?"

"I love slicing," said Kyle. "I help my mom in the kitchen all the time."

Uncle Augustus slammed the junk drawer shut. "So much for the tape measure. I'm heading up to my room to get into character."

He'd been cultivating a great mustache since the previous

party, which also happened to be the last time the enchanted circle in the attic had glowed like a sunbeam through crystal and sparked like a fountain of light.

Ninety minutes later, Birdwistell, Professor Kelvin Birdwistell, made his appearance as the first guest. Of course he did because the trio, and Ronda too, wished he would arrive last—or better yet, not at all.

Dressed in a high-lapelled woolen suit indicative of the mid-1800s, a stiff-collared shirt, and a black tie, the philosophy professor (specializing in the French philosopher Alain Touraine, for you brainy types) trundled his roly-poly avian (from the Latin *avis*, meaning "bird") body into the kitchen. *Imagine a sweet, fat little ruffly sparrow. Now make it human, only not at all sweet and extra fat, and you're in all likelihood picturing Birdwistell.*

Most party guests are polite enough not to make a nuisance of themselves with the kitchen crew. After all, punch must be concocted, hors d'oeuvres arranged, and food of all sorts tasted on the off chance that an enemy snuck in with poison. *(I'm always available for that task. Not that anyone takes advantage of my services.)* Birdwistell, however, cares little for such niceties.

He sniffed his beaky little nose, wrinkling it in what appeared to be disgust. It reminded Walter of the look on his Auntie Max's face after she ingested an entire box of coconut macaroons.

Ronda reappeared in the kitchen. She was now dressed to serve wearing a black cocktail dress, and her warm brown curls were fashioned in a fancy updo. *(Marie Antoinette would have been moss green with envy.)* Pointing to the kitchen door, she said, "Back where you came from, Birdwistell. We have plenty of vegetarian options, so go on your way."

Birdwistell's eyes glittered. "Young lady—"

"I'm not one of your students. Go!"

At the last party, the rude professor had overstepped his bounds with Ronda for the final time.

Father Lou expelled a low whistle *(not a bird whistle, mind you)* as the professor quickly exited the kitchen. "Well done, Ronda."

She pointed her knife at the priest. "You're only saying that because we're going out. I was hardly turning the other cheek, Reverend."

The priest laughed and then tightened his silver ponytail. "You got me. Anything else you need me to do?"

"It's all under control. Thank you, Lou."

"I'm out, then. There's a vestry (church committee) meeting tonight."

"Can I stay for the party?" asked Kyle, after Father Lou had gone.

"Will you be my kitchen helper?" Ronda asked. "I could use an expert slicer like you at the ready."

"Yeah!" he said, ready for the next task.

Now dressed in their costumes, Walter, Linus, and Ophelia lifted their silver serving trays and pressed forward, first serving the guests gathered in the bookstore, and then those sitting around the back garden. Aunt Portia wafted among them, not giving a fig, as usual, for her brother's costume requirements. While she wore a lime green, floor-length dress of the time period—the waist nipped and the sleeves tight around her arms—she had raided her costume jewelry collection and loaded up her arms with bracelets, her neck and bosom with glittering pendants and strings of pearls and jewels of all colors, not to mention the largest and maybe even the most sparkly pair of dangle earrings Ophelia had ever seen. She looked like a nineteenth-century disco ball as she circled the room to greet her guests. Ophelia wondered if she'd ever be as magnificent as Ronda and Aunt Portia.

After most of the food had been devoured, Uncle Augustus, wearing a white linen suit and a black bow tie, rose to give his monologue. Finished with their serving work, the trio of teenagers gratefully retreated to the attic. Watching a relative perform a monologue was embarrassing and awkward at best, unquestionably excruciating at worst.

Perhaps you have a relation who thinks he or she can play the violin so well and then volunteers to provide special music in front of the church at least once a month—even though it sounds like fighting cats when he or she plays. If so, you know what I mean.

They delivered Kyle to his room at The Pierce School so his caretaker, a pleasant young woman named Nan, could ready him for bed. Only an hour remained until 11:11.

As Ophelia relaxed on the floor in the middle of the enchanted circle, Walter dropped for a set of push-ups, and Linus settled himself on the sofa.

"So we're all agreed then." Ophelia crossed her hands over her stomach. "Tom Sawyer this time."

Walter stood. "Let's see how we handle a kid like him.

After Captain Ahab and the Countess de Winter, a boy should be easy."

Obviously, Walter had never read *The Adventures of Tom Sawyer*.

Ophelia winced at his words. Was Walter ever in for a surprise.

four

Some Quandaries Are Merely Huge Problems in Disguise

or Ophelia Doesn't Necessarily Think of Everything

Ophelia discovered the secret of the enchanted circle quite by accident. While innocently reading *The Hunchback of Notre Dame* in the attic one evening, her eyelids decided a brief vacation was necessary. The comfortable blue couch with the gold fringe must have conspired with her eyelids because Ophelia fell asleep. And then the novel slipped from her fingertips and landed just inside the circle.

That happened three 11:11s ago, and the thrill of that first time they'd watched the circle pulsate through the light spectrum, like it was doing presently, never dwindled (lessened). Of course, they all knew what to expect by now. But watching the brilliant green turn into a host of blues, then purples and violets, and pinks and reds and oranges and yellows (imagine autumn leaves in all of their glorious hues glowing and winking) exhilarated them anew.

Upon completing the rainbow, the circle emanated the purest of white lights. *(Nothing akin to those anemic (weak) new Christmas lights that people have taken to using in the past few years. Oh, the horrors of those eerie things. And at*

Christmas too!) The most exciting part arrived next: great fountains of sparks sprayed toward the ceiling as if nozzles were pushed through the floorboards.

"It never gets old," Ophelia whispered to the boys.

"Never," said Linus, his light blue eyes reflecting the scene before him.

"And it always amazes me that it doesn't incinerate (burn) the attic," said Walter.

They laughed as the sparks ceased, leaving a cloud of smoke behind that gathered itself in a twist and then disappeared with a snap. *If you've ever snapped a towel, you'd recognize the sound.*

But the most fantastic part of the event happened inside the circle. Curled up dead center rested one of the cutest little boys *(don't let his looks fool you)* that Ophelia had ever seen. Tom Sawyer, with mud on his clothes and a soft snore on his pink lips, looked as if he had been asleep for days.

"Asleep? Already?" asked Walter, disappointed.

Ophelia knelt down next to Tom. "I figured with his still being a child, we didn't want to scar him with the journey between Book World and Real World. So we fetched him while he was asleep." She lowered her voice. "Actually, I tried something new this time." She leaned over and grabbed the book. Flipping to the last page, she handed the book to Walter. "I'm surprised it worked, to be honest."

The boys examined the page. Just before THE END, Ophelia had written in black ink, AND TOM SAWYER, AFTER A DAY SPENT PLAYING IN THE WOODS, FELL ASLEEP.

Walter chuckled. "Brilliant, O. J.! But why?"

Ophelia liked that Walter had taken to calling her by her initials. "There's a life-and-death situation he needs to take care of."

"His?" asked Linus.

"No. Injun Joe's."

Linus mouthed the words *Injun Joe*, then said, "Seriously?"

"Engine Joe?" said Walter. "Who is Engine Joe?"

"Injun. Like *Indian*, Walt," said Ophelia. "They didn't exactly use the terms 'Native American' or 'First Nation' back then."

"First Nation?" asked Walter. Clearly he hadn't grasped North American culture as well as he fancied.

Here, my deurs, is a quandary that the modern-day reader might experience when reading literature written long ago. Sometimes the society in which the author lived, or the one in which he or she is writing about, is different from our own. A reader must sometimes simply decide to read on, knowing that at least what they're reading about is authentic. What is considered acceptable by society changes. Someday, a perfectly reasonable first name of a friend, say Brian, might end up being a name for only heaven knows what. But the classics survive for a reason, and the reason varies from book to book.

And (to please your parents) just because someone behaves in a certain manner in a book (even in the Bible or The Lion, the Witch and the Wardrobe*) that does not give you permission to act in the same manner. Ask King David. Ask Edmund.*

Onward!

"What's the deal with this Joe bloke?" asked Walter.

"He died of dehydration and starvation in a cave system." Ophelia stood and stretched her back. "Joe isn't a good person, but nobody should die like that, you know? But Tom needs to know about Joe's death so the need for change becomes important to him."

"Right, then," said Walter, stretching his arms and yawning. "If you're going to let the lad sleep, I'm going for a run before bed."

Walter had signed up for the Kingscross 10K. All of the monies raised were slated for the Bard River Camp for Kids.

"I'll keep watch," said Ophelia.

"Me too," said Linus.

And Tom Sawyer, his head now pillowed and covered by a quilt, slept on.

And on, and on.

"Thank goodness it's Saturday," said Ophelia the next morning.

The twins had slept as they always did. Ophelia, on the sofa, snoozed like Rip Van Winkle. Linus, on the other hand, was in a sleeping bag on the floor. He'd woken up at least ten times during the night, after having strange dreams of breathing under water in a submerged shopping mall, or trying to run in a field where the grass was as sharp as swords.

Genius has its trials, I suppose. Perhaps sleeping on planks that had not been scrubbed in decades had something to do with it. Who knows what germs and filth people dragged in on their shoes . . . what slime, what sickness, what . . .

Moving right along!

Already dressed for the day, the siblings happily rid themselves of their school uniforms for an entire weekend. How did they come to be students at a private school when they had no money? Madrigal Pierce, in gratitude for their catching her no-good pyromaniac brother, had offered them a tuition-free education. (She'd heard about their parents, too, and figured how much could two more students really cost?)

39

"Why isn't he awake yet?" Ophelia checked her watch. It was 7:45 A.M. "I thought kids got up earlier than this."

"They do." Linus knelt down beside Tom just as Walter entered the attic wearing black athletic shorts, a yellow T-shirt that said "Stop Looking at My Shirt," and, as Walter would call them, trainers. (You'd call them running shoes.)

"Still asleep?" Walter asked, wiping the sweat from his face with the hem of his T-shirt. "That's odd."

Ophelia sat on the couch admiring the heightened color of Walter's complexion, the way his hair curled next to his temples with perspiration. *(Ugh!)* "Maybe because there's nothing else written in the book, he'll just stay asleep," she posited (put forth a possible explanation).

"Then let's wake him up!" said Walter, pointing to Linus's glass of water sitting on the lab table. Linus nodded.

"But what if that damages him? What if it makes him fizz away like the Wicked Witch of the West?" she asked.

The thought horrified all three of them. You see, the circle possesses a downside. The traveler must get back inside the circle by 11:11 A.M. on the third day after he or she enters Real World, exactly sixty hours after arrival, in order to make the return trip to Book World. If they don't, well you've just read the terrible consequences straight from the lips of Ophelia. In his detailed notes, Cato Grubbs dubbed it, "dissolving in the acids between the worlds."

Cato also coined the terms Book World *and* Real World, *by the way. Could he not have spent a little more time and employed a bit more imagination? Perhaps* Literaria *and* Presentia, *or* Fictivus *and* Modernia *would have been somewhat intriguing. Of course, he didn't ask for* my *help. No one ever does.*

"You have to try and think about all of the possibilities ahead of time when you conduct an experiment," said Linus, revealing yet another reason for his sleepless nights.

Ophelia screwed up her face. "Thanks, Linus. That's just what I needed right now."

"Well, we can't very well just leave him asleep," said Walter, setting down the glass he'd just drained. "He can't go for sixty hours without water. And if we try to give him some, it would wake him up. So our only choice is to—"

"Wake him up," they all said together.

"Let me." Ophelia joined Linus down on the floor by Tom's side. *He really is a cute little boy*, she thought, touching his tousled hair and cherubic (angelic) face. But in this case, she knew looks could be deceiving, as the old saying goes.

She placed her hand on Tom's shoulder and shook it, just barely.

Not a movement, not a peep.

A little harder this time.

Nope.

She turned to her brother. "Oh no! What if I can't wake him at all?"

Walter decided enough was enough. They could postulate (make guesses) the morning away if somebody didn't do something. He clapped his hands next to the boy's head, shouting, "Oy! Oy, mate!"

Ophelia winced. Linus jolted with a start, and Tom Sawyer opened his eyes.

A Reaction Like No Other Requires an Opposite and Equal Reaction Much the Same

or Why "Let Sleeping Dogs Lie" Is Good Advice . . . for the Most Part

The boy jumped to his feet without hesitation. Walter followed suit.

Tom balled his small hands into fists and took a wild shot, aiming for Walter's nose. But the wily (tricky) Brit easily deflected the blow, hooking Tom's wrist with his hand in one movement. In a split second he'd spun the boy around and locked him smoothly in a choke hold.

Thank you, Mr. Yang! he thought.

Ophelia shrieked. "Walter! You're hurting him!"

"Nah. He can still breathe. Can't you, Tom?"

"Why you! I'll git you!" Tom started wriggling like a toddler who wants to be put down.

"See?" said Walter in a calm voice. "Now Tom, I'm bigger than you, stronger than you, and most likely a better fighter than you. If I let you go, do you promise not to punch me again?"

Tom paused a second, then nodded his head as best he could given Walter's forearm under his chin.

Walter let go. Tom stepped forward, and then he wheeled around and punched with more speed than accuracy. But not enough of either, for Walter had him back in a choke hold even quicker than the first time.

Real-life application, he thought. *Brilliant! Thank you again, Mr. Yang.* And he hadn't so much as hurt a hair on Tom's head.

Walter and Tom repeated this little dance again and again until by the fifth time, Walter finally took Tom down to the ground.

Ophelia, feeling as irritated as a blistered heel stuffed inside a brand-new shoe, stomped her foot. "Enough!" she cried. Then she leaned over Tom and shook her finger in his face. "Look here, young man. Get a clue. If he lets you go, it means he isn't going to hurt you. What part of this don't you understand?"

Tom's eyes grew wide and he nodded, swallowing his anger.

"Let him go, Walt," she said.

Walter eased up slowly and Tom stayed put. He reached out a hand and helped the boy to his feet.

"Good," Ophelia said. "That's Walter. I'm Ophelia. And the tall guy there is my brother Linus."

Tom looked around him, taking note of his surroundings for the first time since he'd woken up. Confusion passed across his eyes like storm clouds in a stiff wind. "Where am I? This ain't like any place I ever seen."

Ophelia winced at his horrendous grammar. *(And who can blame her?)*

Surely I can do something about that *in the next two days*, she thought.

Linus read her mind.

Poor Tom.

"I have ever seen," Ophelia corrected.

"You ever seen what?" asked Tom, bewildered.

"And it's not *ain't*. It's *isn't*," Ophelia said slowly, annunciating each syllable.

"What ain't what?" asked Tom. "Are you crazy?"

Linus stifled a bark of laughter with his hand.

She sighed and tried again, "It's not 'I ever seen,' Tom. It's 'I *have* ever seen.' Your grammar is atrocious!" (Even worse than horrendous.)

Oh great, thought Linus. *Ophelia is going to be even bossier than usual.*

Walter was thinking the same thing. When the other fictional characters had traveled through the enchanted circle, they'd always learned something in the process—something important, like matters of love and honor, life and death. But if Ophelia, cute as she may be, had brought Tom over to Real World to teach him better grammar, then the next couple of days promised to be a real snooze.

"You a teacher?" Tom crossed his arms in front of his chest.

"Are you a student?" Ophelia answered him with a question, a sure sign of a teacher if ever there was one.

"When Aunt Polly makes me."

"Well, you have to be one now, Tom. Because in the next two days, you have an awful lot to learn."

"Like what?" He jutted out his chin.

And Linus believed he would have no trouble liking this kid!

"Like how you woke up here in the first place. Let's get you cleaned up so we can eat."

Tom pressed a hand to his stomach. "I am powerful hungry."

"Then follow me."

Ophelia led him out of the room.

Walter threw himself on the couch. "This adventure isn't going to be an adventure after all, mate. More like a nanny job for Ophelia."

"Yep." Linus sat at his lab table.

"Still trying to bring items over from Book World?" Walter asked.

"Yep. And they keep disappearing after a while."

The previous month, Linus had summoned "the one ring to rule them all" through the portal (from Tolkien's The Lord of the Rings trilogy). Unfortunately, an item can only be brought through once, no matter how many copies of the book exist. *In essence, Linus managed to materialize an object so priceless to so many people who wish Middle Earth were real (and some who might actually believe it to be so) only to have it disappear for all eternity! I certainly wouldn't want that on my conscience!*

Thank goodness Ophelia helped him choose less precious items for further experimentation: the crumbled wedding cake of Miss Havisham in *Great Expectations* (inedible, of course), the wedding cake from *Sense and Sensibility* (not bad), and the pudding from *A Christmas Carol*. Feeling a little homesick that day, Walter had suggested it. It was delicious.

"What do you think the problem is, mate?" Walter asked. He was more like Ophelia in the brain department. He loved to read. However, subjects like science, especially chemistry, felt like a foreign language to him. But he knew how important it is for people to talk things out. Solutions come more easily that way.

"I don't know. The outside temperature? Knowing Cato, it probably has to be either eleven degrees Celsius or Farenheit."

"Or both."

"Yeah . . ."

Walter looked outside at the perfect September day. It was seventy-five degrees, the sky displaying a deeper, cleaner blue that only an autumn day can rally. "It could be a while."

"Yeah. But in the meantime, we can eat well."

"I'd fancy some of that chowder from *Moby-Dick*," said Walter. "The only problem is that even if you stuff yourself full, fifteen minutes later you're hungry again."

Linus laughed. "Disappearing food."

"The new diet fad. We could make a fortune," Walter said. It trumped (beat) picking pockets.

Once again, the flushing toilet was quite the cause for fascination. Tom, like Quasimodo, Captain Ahab, and the Countess de Winter, couldn't get enough of it. Ophelia tried not to think of the ecological disaster they might be causing.

"Look at this, Tom." She ran her hand under the spigot filling the tub with water. "It's warm!"

Tom sucked in his breath. "And it's coming out of the *wall*!"

"Pretty cool, huh?"

He put his hand under the stream. "No, it's warm."

Ophelia laughed. "Good one. Now I'm going to find you some clean clothes while you take a bath." She turned off the water. "You get on in."

Tom took the soap she offered. "Aww, all right, I reckon. But only 'cause I'm powerful hungry."

Her hand paused on the doorknob. "And don't worry about washing your hair."

Walter and Linus would have applauded her decision not to make Tom's transition more difficult than need be; I, on the other hand, wonder if she's lost her mind.

six

More Missing Books and a Surprisingly Good Speller

or If It Isn't Where You Put It, Chances Are Somebody Else Did Something with It Because It Could Never Be Your Own Fault, Now Could It?

Ophelia set a plate of fried ham, scrambled eggs, and wheat toast in front of a thoroughly scrubbed Tom Sawyer. He'd found the shampoo and washed his hair by accident. And a can of shaving cream ended up all over his body—and the bathroom as well. Linus was out purchasing a new can as Ophelia made breakfast, hoping Uncle Augustus would be none the wiser.

Aunt Portia and Ophelia had painted the kitchen a brilliant lime green a couple of weeks before. The cabinets were now a citrusy yellow, and all of the wooden chairs had been painted their own bright colors: sunset orange, strawberry, plum, petal pink, lavender, and aquamarine.

Aunt Portia entered the kitchen and sat next to Tom *(who'd chosen to sit in the plum chair, by the way).* "Well, well! Who have we here?" she trilled. *When somebody trills, they're speaking in a higher tone than usual. So that puts Portia's normally high voice somewhere near Sirius (the brightest star in the night sky).*

51

Ophelia reached into the refrigerator and pulled out a jug of milk. "Oh, it's just Tom Sawyer," she said nonchalantly (casually, as if what she was talking about was a boring, everyday occurrence like watching cartoons or playing video games).

Aunt Portia clapped her hands, and her abundant rings jangled together like pennies in a coin purse. "Well, how utterly delightful!" She turned to Tom and laid a hand on his arm. He regarded her as one regards a force of nature, intriguing but uncontrollable. "So tell me, Tom. Is Becky Thatcher as pretty as everyone says?"

If her question surprised Tom, he didn't show it. "Oh, yes ma'am! Prettier even! She's just about the prettiest girl you ever saw!"

"Seen," said Ophelia. "You've ever seen."

"Seen," repeated Tom. "S-E-E-N. Seen."

Aunt Portia giggled.

Ophelia procured a glass from the cabinet over the sink. "That's not helping, Aunt Portia. That boy's grammar is atrocious."

"Atrocious," said Tom. "A-T-R-O-C-I-O-U-S. Atrocious."

"Well, you can't say that about his spelling, Ophelia. Would you mind frying me up a piece of that ham?"

"Not at all." Ophelia poured the milk and set the glass by Tom's plate. "Why do you keep spelling everything?"

"Is you my teacher or ain't you?" Tom chugged half of the cold milk.

"*Are* you my teacher or *aren't* you?" corrected Ophelia, dragging out the platter of leftover party ham from the fridge yet again. She remembered watching Walter slice it and felt her heart warm.

"I ain't your teacher!"

Aunt Portia giggled again.

"Well?" asked Tom.

Ophelia peeled the cellophane off the plate and stabbed two pieces of ham with a serving fork. "I guess so. Yes. Yes, I am your teacher."

"Then if you don't care about my spelling, I reckon nobody else will give a nevermind what I says, either ways."

Ophelia had absolutely no idea what to do with that sentence. She arranged the ham slices in the cast iron pan.

Thankfully, Aunt Portia came to the rescue, albeit with unsettling news. "Four more books were missing this morning. I have no idea what to do."

"Really?" asked Ophelia. "So many people were here for the party. Do you think it could have been one of the guests?"

"Heavens, I hope not!"

"Or maybe the burglar was using the party as cover," Ophelia suggested.

"Now, that I can believe," said Aunt Portia.

Tom looked up from his food. "You got you a thief afoot in these parts?"

Ophelia let that slide. "Yes, unfortunately."

"I knowed a thief once. Stole all sorts of things. Likker. Treasure. Most everything."

"Injun Joe?" asked Ophelia.

Tom slapped the table. "Don't tell me you know 'im too? Well, I reckon I must not be too far from home, then."

"I know way more than you think and a whole lot more than you'd like, Tom Sawyer." Ophelia flipped the ham.

By the time Aunt Portia's ham finished cooking, Tom's plate was cleaner than my kitchen sink. *(I just employed what is called hyperbole or exaggeration.* Nothing *is cleaner than my kitchen sink.)*

Tom perched on Ophelia's favorite park bench and gazed out over the Bard River. The water, reflecting the trees on its banks and the sky overhead, rambled along at a slower pace knowing that cold weather was just around the corner.

Just a moment. Let's be honest, shall we? That river didn't know any such thing. I was employing a literary device known as personification. *Another fancy word for this concept is* anthropomorphism. *Say that three times fast! This concept means one assigns human qualities to otherwise nonhuman objects. A good example of this is the saying, "Even the walls have ears." I cannot speak for your walls, but mine can't hear a blessed thing. It simply means, "Be careful what you say; anybody and everybody could be listening in." If you ever find yourself trapped in the pages of George Orwell's dystopian novel (a story set in a world no sane person would wish to inhabit) titled* 1984, *you'll know precisely what I mean.*

Ophelia had just tried her best to explain Tom's current situation.

"I ain't *real?*" he asked.

"Of course you are. As real as I am. See?" She ran her hand over her bare forearm, then Tom's. He'd been delighted by the fashions of the day: comfy shorts and a soft T-shirt with short sleeves. "A feller could get used to such," he'd said with a grin after his bath.

"I don't reckon I'm real if I started in the mind of a book writer—ouch!"

Ophelia had pinched his arm. "See?" she said.

He glared at her, rubbing the sore spot.

"So let's have as much fun as we can until you have to go back. Okay?"

Tom slumped down on the bench and crossed his arms over his bony chest. "I reckon. I ain't going to give you no lip about it, neither."

"I'm not going to give you any lip about it."

Tom wondered if he'd ever use a state of being verb again. Only he didn't think of it in those words exactly. A state of being verb merely implies existence. Am. Is. Was. Were. *Can you am? Can you is? Can you was? Can you were? You cannot help but do so! Terrific, isn't it? Your mom might say, "Why are you sitting around doing nothing?" Well, you can confidently know that you're busy just being. It may not seem like much, but it certainly beats the alternative. (Think about it.)*

"And you say I get to go home?"

"Yes. The day after tomorrow."

"I reckon it'll be fine." He leaned over, picked up a pebble, and hurled it into the Bard.

"Let's go see Father Lou," said Ophelia.

Just then, the angry shouting of older boys drew their attention toward the middle of the park.

"A fight!" Tom sprung to his feet and sprinted forward in such a flash that Ophelia had no time to catch him.

"Tom! Don't!" she cried, hoping to grab him before he picked up a big sack of trouble.

Impossible.

Tom Sawyer had perfected the art of being "almost caught." In other words, he could ascertain (figure out) the very last second before getting away, and he could run faster than almost anybody in St. Petersburg (Missouri, not Russia), his hometown. *(Mark Twain doesn't say so; I just like to think that he could.)*

"Beware The Black Avenger of the Spanish Main!" he cried, flinging himself into the fray without a moment's hesitation.

Ophelia dabbed a wet washcloth over the angry abrasion on Tom's forehead. "Your tussle with Walter should have given you a clue, Tom."

Walter nodded, sitting on the edge of the tub. "Those blokes were almost twice your age, mate."

"Much obliged to you, Walter," Tom said, perched on the closed lid of the commode (toilet).

Using his martial arts skills, Walter had broken up the fight without hurting anybody too seriously. Tom had provided the chance he'd been waiting for since joining Mr. Yang's class. He pushed playfully at the side of Tom's head.

"Clearly, they weren't playing at pirates," said Ophelia.

Tom winced. "If Joe had been there . . ." Tom was referring to his best friend Joe Harper, a.k.a. (also known as) The Terror of the Seas.

"We'd be cleaning him up too," said Ophelia. She laid aside the washcloth. "There! Almost as good as new."

"Notwithstanding the black eye he'll have when he wakes up tomorrow," said Walter. "If you're absolutely keen on getting into fights, mate, come get me first."

"Sounds like a mighty good idea." Tom rubbed a tender spot on the back of his head.

"You have to give him credit, though," Ophelia said, gathering up the first aid supplies, "he hung in there for a long time, considering how little he is."

"I ain't little." Tom sulked.

"Aren't. Aren't little." Ophelia left the bathroom.

Walter's eyes met Tom's.

"She always so bossy?" asked Tom.

"I'm afraid so, mate. You'll get used to it. You have to. Or else it will drive you crazy." Walter paused and thought about the Ophelia he'd come to know. "She really does care, which is why she's like that. You know anybody like that?"

Tom nodded. "Aunt Polly. She's even worse than that girl. And less pretty."

"Pretty helps, doesn't it?"

Sigh.

"Well, here we are again, Ophelia darling!" said Aunt Portia as the two sat in folding chairs for another community meeting.

The last time there'd been such a meeting, a wildcat was on the loose. Nobody ever spotted the big cat again after that, thereby disclosing the pointlessness of most meetings. A little time, some patience, and most problems tend to resolve themselves. That is, unless germs come into play. Now for those matters—the sooner we can meet, the better. I'll cheerfully provide refreshments!

Professor Birdwistell lowered himself next to Aunt Portia. *(Knowing Birdwistell, to say he* lowered himself *didn't exclusively refer to his body movement, but also his attitude that such a meeting was beneath him.)* He regarded the metal folding chair with disdain.

"Portia," he said with a sniff and an upward lift of his chins.

"Well, hello, Kelvin!" she answered with her prevailing

exuberance (cheerfulness). Aunt Portia consistently nourishes a hopeful inclination for every person and every situation (she thinks the best of others). "What brings you here?"

He laughed, the disdain from his expression now transferred to his voice. "I should imagine it's the same matter that brings *you* here," he said with a supercilious (arrogant, snobby) sniff.

"Have you a cold, dear?" Aunt Portia asked.

Ophelia stifled a laugh with her hand.

"Why, no. Of course not! The Birdwistells are a hearty lot, madam."

"Oh, it's miss, not madam. Allergies, then? You have me a bit worried, what with all of the sniffing you do."

"No allergies either, thank you very much."

"A nervous tic?" she asked.

Ophelia shot up from her seat and raced out into the hallway of the basement at All Souls Episcopal Church, where the meeting was being held. She was bent double and holding her sides in silent gales of amusement when Father Lou rushed up and placed a concerned hand on the back of her head.

"Ophelia! Are you all right?"

Father Lou is someone who asks such questions sincerely. He doesn't ask, "How are you doing?" and then become impatient when you fail to answer the expected "Fine" or "Busy!" Rather, Father Lou truly wants to know your present state, and that makes him either a saint or very nosy. Ronda chalks it up to a mixture of the two.

"I'm all right. I just had to get out of there!" She gulped down another burst of laughter. "My aunt was doing a number on Birdwistell."

"Like Ronda did at the party?"

"Oh no! As only Aunt Portia can do and still get away with it!"

Father Lou peered inside the room. "I wonder what brings him here?" He tightened his ponytail and smoothed his priestly gray shirt.

Ophelia started laughing all over again.

"I have a job for you," he said, "if that's okay with you."

A minute later, Father Lou called the meeting to order and invited participants to speak. Some expressed their fear, others felt angry; but all felt disconcerted that there had been no sign of forced entry.

"We need to determine a common theme here—other than antiques, of course," Father Lou said. "I'd like everyone to make a list of the stolen items and the names of people who've been in your home recently. Ophelia?"

Ophelia passed out sheets of paper and stubby yellow pencils that assumed you would make no mistakes. *(No erasers.)*

"In the meantime," said Father Lou, "I'd encourage all of you to batten down the hatches and be on the lookout. After you've finished your list, just leave it on the table by the door. Please help yourself to some refreshments at the back of the room."

Of course.

Through no fault of her own, Clarice Yardly-Poutsmouth was forced to learn the secret of the enchanted attic just a month ago. She'd watched as the Countess de Winter, d'Artagnan, and all three musketeers returned to 1600s France.

She was not impressed.

In fact, she wanted nothing to do with the characters traveling from Book World to Real World and back again. "I'd rather play tennis," she decided. But as Linus's girlfriend, she sought to be supportive of his scientific endeavors and his latest experiments with literary travel. Linus was just as glad she didn't care about the circle. It made it easier not to have her involved, and she was far less likely than most people to blab about it to others.

With her long blond hair gathered into a messy bun and still wearing her soccer uniform after The Pierce School's win over Princeton High that morning, Clarice now sat on the blue sofa while working on a social studies group project. "Why do teachers assign group projects when only one person does all of the work? They do know that, don't they?" she complained. *And who can blame her!*

Sitting at the lab table on the other side of the attic, Linus scribbled a note to his cousin, mentor, and sometimes nemesis (arch enemy), Cato Grubbs:

Cousin Cato,
Do you have anything to do with these burglaries?
Just trying to give credit where credit is due.
                    Linus Easterday

He placed the note between the pages of Cato's own publication *Trapdoors to Other Realms*, and then turned to Clarice. "Hot dog?"

Clarice stood up. "Absolutely."

They visited their favorite stand over at Paris Park and consumed three dogs each, serious about doing their bit to keep Mr. Bolwecki in business. *Enjoy that kind of fast metabolism while you're blessed with it, my dears, because soon enough even* looking *upon a donut will add girth to your frame (make you gain weight).*

While Ophelia attended the community meeting and Linus sent notes and ate hot dogs with his pretty girlfriend, Walter escorted Tom around the school. The equipment in the lab fascinated Tom. "It's like that table in the attic!"

"Which, let me warn you, you are never to touch," Walter said. "Linus is easygoing enough, but don't touch his work."

They progressed down the hall into another classroom. "This is the math room," said Walter.

"You got different classrooms for different subjects?" Tom stood in the middle of Mr. Harper's room. "This room is just for cipherin'?" (Arithmetic.)

"Yes. We're also divided by grade level, as well."

"We got just one big room."

"That's the way it was back then."

"A feller sure can get in a heap more trouble that way." Tom rubbed his backside without thinking.

"Things have changed in that regard too. Teachers don't hit students anymore."

"Is that so? I reckon things get outta hand!"

"Not really."

Tom looked confused, then shrugged. "I reckon you'd know." He patted the desk chair. "What's this here stuff?"

"Plastic." *(Where was Linus when you needed a good explanation? Walter's description of plastic had left Tom utterly befuddled (confused).)*

As they left the computer lab, Madrigal Pierce materialized (suddenly appeared). Her Saturday clothes looked just like all her others: Long skirt, high heels, crisp blouse, and the requisite shawl.

"Walter! Who is this? And what is he doing in the school? You haven't requested an authorized visit."

And then Walter lied. I can't put it any other way. I will say, however, that he made it believable.

"Ms. Pierce, this is Kyle's cousin, Tom. He's made a surprise visit this weekend. He's interested in attending school here, and Kyle asked me to show him around while he finishes up his math homework."

Madrigal pursed her lips, not fooled for a moment, but too tired to make an issue of it. She'd been up late the night before helping Ronda clean up after the big party. "Just finish up quickly, Walter."

"Thank you, ma'am," Walter said.

She clicked away down the hall.

"Who's Kyle?" asked Tom.

"Your new cousin. I'll take you to meet him."

When Tom and Kyle met each other, both felt as though they'd found a long lost friend. As Mark Twain himself put it, they were "two souls with a single thought."

Have you ever met someone and right away you knew you'd found what some people call "a kindred spirit"? It isn't ten minutes into your encounter before you feel like you've known this person all of your life. The conversation flows without impediment (hindrance, obstacle) and you agree on so many things. You're a night owl. So are they! They like roller coasters. So do you! They believe reality television is a blight upon the human race and could quite possibly be the downfall of our civilization. Obviously, you feel that way as well.

Well, Tom Sawyer had no idea that reality TV shows existed. Still doesn't, much to my relief. Imagine taking that sort of behavior back to the 1800s. You might be thrust into the nervous hospital, and if that isn't telling . . . ahem. Now, where were we?

Walter had sternly warned Tom not to reveal his true identity to anyone. While he could make it known that he was from Missouri and talk about his friends and family, under no circumstances was he to divulge so much as a word about Mark Twain or the 1800s in general. Bearing in mind his scuffle in the attic with Walter, Tom readily agreed.

Kyle showed Tom his rock collection. Tom admired the glittering amethyst crystals in Kyle's favorite geode. Tom recounted the adventures of his campouts along the Mississippi River with Joe and Huck. Walter stopped breathing at the mention of those names, but the two chattered on, bouncing like spring crickets from subject to subject. Clearly, Kyle wasn't as well versed in literature as he was proficient in mathematics. *Normally, I would not view this favorably. But in this case, thank goodness!*

Tom stood and returned the geode to the shelf above the desk. He pointed at Kyle's wheelchair. "What's that for?"

"It's my legs most of the time."

Tom didn't understand. "What do you mean?"

"I can't walk." Kyle zeroed in on Tom's face, ready for all the fun to pack up and leave in the twinkling of an eye. *(Personification and an allusion to Saint Paul! I must be on a roll!)*

"Why, that's awful!" Tom plopped down on the bed next to Kyle.

"It's not so bad." Kyle reached for the arm of his spiffy black set of wheels and then hefted himself onto the seat. He positioned his feet on the platforms designed to hold them, and then spun the chair around the center of the room. "Maybe someday you can take it for a spin. Down in the park."

Tom figured that would be a heap of fun and said so.

seven

Owls Aren't the Only Creatures Who Stay Up Late

or If You're Going to Wander Around after Lights Out, Don't Forget Your Chalk

Ophelia pulled one of Linus's beanies over Tom's hair. "There. Now nobody will see you in the dark."

"Stealth," said Linus, looking like Tom's older brother. Both wore black sweatpants, a black hoodie, and dark beanies. "Ready, kid?"

"I reckon I am!" Excitement jangled through Tom's limbs. Linus had won Tom over earlier that afternoon with a walk around Kingscross, explaining how cars, among other things, work.

"So they're akin to steamboats on wheels," said Tom, "only not powered by steam, but some kind of water. What was it again?"

"Gasoline," answered Linus.

"You're much better at s'plainin' than that other boy," Tom said.

Linus, relying on steamboats to explain electricity, too, was surprised at how Tom picked up a basic grasp of our more rudimentary technology with little effort. "A quick study," he told Ophelia later.

"Not surprising. He's the leader of his friend group and has an inventive, creative mind," she informed him.

Courageous too, she thought as the trio and their smaller charge skulked (sneaked) across the school basement to the mouth of the not-so-secret tunnel. Ophelia rooted in her jacket pocket. "I've got several pieces of chalk this time and extra batteries, just in case."

Linus held up the water bottle dangling from his fingers.

Walter patted his pocket, indicating that he'd completed his task of preparing for their expedition. "Energy bars at the ready—if need be," he said.

Nobody wanted "if need be," except maybe Tom. But he knew better than anyone that a person could get lost in a cave and still be found.

"Did you leave the note?" asked Walter.

"I did," said Ophelia. "It's on my nightstand."

If they lost their way, somebody needed to know the specific vicinity of their disappearance. A general vanishing would do no one any good.

It does my heart proud to think of young people employing that much common sense. Hopefully, you are of the same ilk (kind)—unlike many of the reality TV dullards who parade their nincompoop selves across television screens today. (I simply love the word nincompoop. *Don't you?)*

"You sure you're okay to go in with us, mate?" asked Walter.

"We got McDougal's Cave back home. I probably know them as good—"

"As well," interrupted Ophelia.

"—as *well* as anybody. Except for Injun Joe maybe, but ..." His gaze dropped to the floor, and he shoved his hands deep in the pockets of his pants. "I ain't skeered, if that's what you're worried about."

"I'm *not* scared," said Ophelia.

The rumor mill of The Pierce School had provided everyone with the news that the tunnel was to be sealed on Monday. "In any case," said Walter, "it's now or never."

Walter led the group and Linus brought up the rear, leaving Tom and Ophelia sandwiched between the two older boys. Ophelia kept her right hand on Tom's shoulder.

"You think we'll find a secret lair?' asked Tom, about three minutes in.

Ophelia laughed. "I doubt it. Criminals don't seem to use places like this for hideouts anymore." She further contemplated the thought. "Well, I don't know why they don't, really. It would make sense."

Walter agreed. "You'd think people would take advantage of locations like this more often. Who would think to look for stolen goods hidden in nature?" Walter, though a reformed pickpocket and petty thief, still possessed the reasoning skills of one. "It would be brilliant, really. Providing the entrance is kept a secret."

"There's your problem," said Linus.

"People have a hard time with that." Ophelia squeezed Tom's shoulder. "And some secrets should never be secrets in the first place."

He whipped his head around to look at her, shocked. "You know 'bout that?"

"Uh-huh."

"Well, how do you like that? You was tellin' the truth when you said you knowed everything."

"Don't tell her that," said Linus before Ophelia could correct Tom. "She'll never let us forget it."

They arrived at the larger tunnel. Ophelia drew an arrow on the tunnel wall, pointing back in the direction from which they'd come. "Right or left?" she asked.

They shrugged.

"I'm feeling left, then," she said. "If I'm not mistaken, going to the right will lead us further into town, and the left will take us out toward the country."

Nobody really agreed or disagreed, having no theories of their own on the matter.

So left they went, remaining in the same formation.

As they walked along for five more minutes, Tom trailed his hand along the hewn limestone walls. "These ain't no caves," he said.

"These *aren't* caves," said Ophelia.

"He's right," Linus agreed, as they came to a stop.

The older boys shone their flashlights all around.

"Definitely tunnels," said Walter. "I mean, we knew that. I just thought it would lead to a cave."

"What do you think these tunnels were for?" Ophelia asked.

"Dunno," said Walter. "But whatever it was, the Pierce family must have had something to do with it."

They continued exploring, leaving chalk arrows every so often to mark the return path. Side corridors dumped into the principal path they explored.

"Do you think they go to other houses?" asked Ophelia. What an intriguing find! Her story-loving mind switched on; but here in the dark, she could only conjure giant hamsters running about a stone maze.

"Don't know that either." Walter stopped. "I say we just forge ahead on this path. It's getting wider and wider. And there's a slight incline too."

"I noticed," said Linus.

"What time is it?" Walter turned and shone his light on Ophelia.

She checked her watch in the beam of Walter's flashlight. "Twelve-thirty."

"Seriously?" asked Linus.

"Time gets powerful funny underground," Tom informed them.

"He should know," said Ophelia. "Tom and Becky Thatcher were lost in McDougal's Cave for several days. Most of St. Petersburg, Missouri, thought they were dead. And they'd put forth quite a search too."

"It was a heap a fun at first. Then we got skeered. But I had to be brave for Becky. Somebody's got to stay brave at times like that."

Ophelia admired Tom for keeping his wits about him, and she told him so.

He replied, "Aww, shucks. You'd a done the same thing."

"You would have done the same thing," corrected Ophelia.

"Let's try for the end of this passage," said Walter, "and see where we end up."

"Lead the way, intrepid trailblazer," said Ophelia.

Walter grinned and moved forward.

Forty minutes later, their fingers and noses tipped with chill, the path widened and dumped them into—

"A cave!" said Walter, the light from his flashlight melting away in the larger space.

"A real cave!" Tom cried.

"Finally," said Linus, shining his light as well.

The four of them still stood in a line, no longer front to back, but side by side.

"Wow." Ophelia circled her flashlight beam around the space, adding her light to the others'. "Look!" she said, halting the beam on a set of empty metal shelves, a bedroll on a cot, and a kerosene lamp.

Walter whistled. "So we're not the only ones who know about this place."

As the younger set says, "Thank you, Captain Obvious."

"Look!" Tom pointed to a large opening in the far wall.

They proceeded toward it and soon stood at the mouth of the cave. Hanging vines veiled the entry. Walter drew them aside like a curtain.

The moon, small, clear, and brighter than all three flashlights combined, illumined the silver water coursing before them.

"The Bard," said Linus.

"I don't like it." Walter pointed his flashlight just outside the cave's mouth. "Something feels wrong. The mud of the banks has been recently disturbed, and look." He shone the beam at their feet. "Muddy footprints. Several sets."

"And what are those shelves for?" Ophelia wondered.

"Pirates!" cried Tom. "I knowed it!"

"I knew it. And there aren't any pirates around here," said Ophelia.

Maybe in Somalia, thought Linus.

"Although they have them in Somalia," Ophelia said, wondering where she'd read that fact.

"Where's that?" asked Tom.

"Africa." Linus scratched his head through his beanie.

"This is a mystery for sure," said Walter.

"Maybe if we find out the reason for the tunnels, we might get a clue." Ophelia looked up and down the river. "We're not far from the dam."

"We'd better get back." Walter turned and led the way back to the passageway.

Five minutes into the return journey, Tom said, "I still think it's pirates."

The others laughed and shoved him playfully.

The fact is, Tom was closer to the truth than any of them.

You see, my dears, sometimes the phrase "older and wiser" need not apply. The trio erroneously (mistakenly) assumed Tom was simply being a fanciful little boy. But none of them had found secret treasure, been lost in a cave system for days, or witnessed a murder. Only Tom Sawyer could make that claim, and that experience surely counts for something.

eight

Those Tickets Ain't Worth Much Around These Parts, Mister

or Colloquialism (Heavily Accented Speech) Becomes Annoying after a While, but Not as Annoying as a Self-Righteous Know-It-All

Tom Sawyer, accustomed to sneaking out at night and having to wake up for school the next morning, awakened at seven, despite a 3 A.M. bedtime.

Ophelia snored on the blue sofa, or I suppose so. *Linus swears she snores like a seventy-year-old man, so why should that night have been any different?*

Tom deemed another trip to Paris Park a fine idea. He decided the black pants and T-shirt he'd slept in were clean enough. *Actually, count that as a leap on my part. The more I ponder, the more I believe Tom Sawyer would not have given one thought to his clothing. Make sure your characters act according to their, well, character.*

Only, Ophelia failed to realize any of that when she awakened at nine o'clock to find Tom Sawyer gone!

She rushed downstairs and checked the bedrooms. Linus sleeping. No Tom.

The panic surging through her veins swept everything

she'd read about Tom Sawyer along with it. She forgot he was wily (street smart) and not given to panic. She forgot he had been out and about on explorations for years. She forgot children were afforded more freedom where he came from.

But she remembered he might forget to look both ways while crossing the street.

Darting out of her bedroom, she ran into Uncle Augustus. "Oh!"

"My dear! What's all this?" He had shaved his mustache, thank goodness.

"Did you see a . . . little boy?"

His eyes, bleached the pale blue of a humid summer sky, sparkled. "I certainly did! And you'll hardly believe what he told me."

As you correctly assume, Aunt Portia knew about the circle. Augustus remained oblivious.

Oh great, thought Ophelia. "I can't wait to hear."

"He said his name is Tom Sawyer. Isn't that de*light*ful? He even claimed to be from Missouri. Too bad *he* wasn't at the soiree!"

Ophelia grasped for something to say. Nothing came to mind.

Uncle Augustus filled in the space. "I asked him if he was a student at The Pierce School. He said yes."

Ophelia blew out a sigh of relief.

"He seems a tad young," Uncle Augustus continued.

"Prodigy!" Ophelia blurted. "Tom's a writing prodigy!"

A prodigy is someone exceedingly excellent in, usually, a particular area, collecting and maintaining skills from early childhood onward of such proficiency that it boggles the minds of ordinary people. Mozart, a prodigy, composed his first symphony at the age of four. Beyond "gifted," prodigies are living miracles, rare specimens of humankind. You, most likely, aren't one of them, but don't let that concern you. You shouldn't be any less proud of your accomplishments.

You see, dear reader, you're a very unique collection of gifts and talents. Add to those the people who love you and the experiences, good and bad, that you've collected over the years, and you are as equipped as any prodigy to fulfill a grand purpose. How was that, Mom and Dad?

If you feel as if you've just consumed a gallon of maple syrup, take it up with the guidance counselor—preferably in a registered letter. Thank you. Call again!

Uncle Augustus raised his eyebrows. "He seemed quite normal to me. A writing prodigy, hmm? His grammar was abysmal." (Extremely or hopelessly bad.)

"Did he say where he was going?" Ophelia prudently (wisely) figured the old saying "the less said, the better" applied to the current circumstances.

"I assume back to the school. Shouldn't you be getting ready for church? Father Lou has invited us over for Sunday dinner afterward."

"I forgot!" Ophelia turned and ran back down the hallway.

"Breakfast in fifteen," he called.

"Not hungry!" she responded.

She dashed into Linus's room. "Wake up!" She poked his shoulder.

Linus opened his eyes. "Seriously?"

"Yes! Tom's gone. Uncle Auggie met him and thinks he goes to school next-door. And Father Lou is having us over for Sunday dinner."

"The connection?" He sat up and reached for the T-shirt he'd cast aside during the night.

"We've got to find Tom before church!" Honcstly, some-times she wondered about her brother's brain. "You don't think the bullies will be around on a Sunday morning, do you?"

"Probably not. You're overreacting."

Ophelia rolled her eyes. "Thank you, Linus Easterday."

"I'll get Walt."

"I'll get changed."

Ophelia felt stupid. The trio stood on the river path watching Tom race Kyle's wheelchair farther down the way.

"I should have come here first before I bothered you guys," she said. "I'm sorry."

"No worries," Walter said. "I wanted to take a run any-way." He broke into a canter toward Tom and Kyle, waving to the boys as he passed.

"They look like they're having fun," she said.

"Yep." Linus, like a lot of insomniacs, got his best sleep between five and nine in the morning. So when somebody wakes him for no reason, well— "They sure do."

"Okay, Mr. Cranky."

A minute later they joined Kyle on the bench where he sat looking as happy as they'd ever seen him.

"Guess what?" he cried. "You'll never believe it!"

"Tell 'em!" said Tom, practically skidding the wheelchair to a stop in front of them.

"I decided to read my literature assignment—"

Please don't let it be The Adventures of Tom Sawyer, Ophelia thought.

"—over there by the playground. And those bullies came around."

Linus looked at Ophelia just in time to see her daggered gaze in his direction. *See?*

"One of them started making fun of me," Kyle continued. "I tried to joke it off. You kinda get used to it. But the smallest of the group—"

"Usually the one with the loudest mouth," said Walter who'd circled back around, his curiosity greater than his need to train.

"Uh-huh. He just kept going. It was getting pretty mean."

Tom jumped to his feet, the wheelchair rolling out from behind him several feet. "And I heard 'em! I knowed what was a-goin' to happen next!"

Linus and Walter looked at Ophelia.

"I knew what was going to happen next," she said anyway.

Kyle nodded wildly. "He sure did! I didn't even know he was around, when all of a sudden he went after that guy! His fists were going like crazy!"

Tom puffed out his chest. "I reckon I'll have me another black eye to match this here one come tomorrow mornin'!"

A deep purple crescent earned in yesterday's fight seemed to hold up his eyeball. Ophelia winced. So much for being good at taking care of children.

Linus worked himself up for the speech. It couldn't be helped. Annoying times sometimes called for equally annoying measures. He leaned against the jamb of the bathroom door. "We've got to call a moratorium (a stop) on all of the grammar correction," he said, willing to speak two pages worth of dialogue if it would shut his sister up.

"Why?" she shot back as she braided her hair for church.

At first they started attending All Souls to be nice to Father Lou. But combine the fact that a former tough-guy priest seasoned his sermons with humor and exciting stories of catching

criminals with the fact that ninety percent of the members were over seventy and passed them candies throughout the service, who wouldn't go back?

Ophelia turned from the bathroom mirror to face her brother, her arms now crossed in front of her and her brown eyes glittering with a challenge. "Are you questioning my teaching methods?"

Tom flushed the toilet again.

"You're not a teacher!" Linus said.

Tom looked up from that fascinating swirl of water. "You ain't?"

"*Aren't.*"

Linus groaned. "Come *on*! Just knock it off, already!" He blew a great gust of air between his lips. "Tom. Aren't you getting sick of being corrected all the time?"

"Aww . . . Ophelia don't mean nothing by it, I suspect."

Ophelia opened her mouth, then closed it.

"Thanks," said Linus.

"How can you stand listening to him, Linus?" she asked.

"Hey! That ain't nice!" said Tom.

"Look, Ophelia. Use your head! He's going to say it regardless. But we won't have to listen to *you* anymore. Give the kid a break, why don't you?"

Tears welled in Ophelia's eyes. "I like you a whole lot better when you keep your own mouth shut, Linus." She pushed past him, beat a path to her room, and slammed the door.

Tom let out a low whistle. "She's worse than Sid, I tell you."

"Who's Sid?"

"My little brother. We live with our Aunt Polly. He's a snitch and a sissy, and I don't like having him around."

Well, at least Ophelia isn't as bad as all that, thought Linus.

"What about it, Tom?" he asked. "Can you clean up your grammar a little? You don't use *ain't* when you're composing sentences in school, do you?"

Tom shook his head. "'Course not."

"Start there. That should take care of half of the problems at least."

"I'll try. I reckon I can do that if I think hard enough."

"Thanks. You ready for church?"

Tom's face bloomed with a mild freak-out *(it's in the dictionary, folks)*. "Where's my coat? I got to find them tickets! I got to win me that Bible!"

"What are you talking about?" asked Linus. Nobody at All Souls had ever won a Bible that he'd ever seen. Maybe Tom knew something about church matters that he didn't. Linus shrugged. "Your coat is up in the attic. I'll get it for you."

Linus, drawing all over the handout they'd received on their way into the sanctuary, gave Tom permission to do the same. While Linus sketched out his ideas for a more aerodynamic wing for what he now realized could be a flying machine for the masses, Tom wrote "Becky" over and over. Ophelia jotted down notes on the sermon. *(Yes, my dears, she is* that *person.)* And Walter tried not to fall asleep. Everyone enjoyed the candy.

After the final prayer, Tom leaned over to Walter. "When can we show our tickets?"

"What tickets, mate?"

Tom dug down into his coat pocket and pulled out a handful of blue, yellow, and red tickets. "They're for memorizing Bible verses."

"You've memorized that many? Brilliant!" Walter whispered. As competitive as most boys his age, he was intrigued. "Any of the others come close to having that many tickets?"

"Not a one." Tom grinned like the Cheshire Cat. *(From* Alice in Wonderland, *another allusion.)*

Ophelia heard the entire conversation. Walter, not having read *The Adventures of Tom Sawyer*, couldn't have known that Tom had traded other valuable objects, such as licorice, fish hooks, and marbles, for tickets earned by the other children. She couldn't wait to see what Father Lou was going to do with this one!

She waited until the priest bade a pleasant good-bye to the last parishioner in the queue (it means "line," and it's pronounced *cue*) that always formed immediately after the service ended.

"Father Lou, this is Tom Sawyer."

"Is it now?" He smiled, unperturbed (not surprised). He'd become aware of the enchanted circle back when Quasimodo, the hunchback of Notre Dame, had journeyed from medieval France to the attic on Rickshaw Street. And he'd lent a hand on all of the adventures that had taken place since. "How are you, Tom? How was the journey?"

Tom jerked his eyes to Walter who nodded. "It's all right, mate. Father Lou knows what's what. We can trust him not to blather about it."

The older lads excused themselves and went outside. Not so Ophelia.

"I reckon it was just fine," answered Tom.

"He was asleep," Ophelia said. "Have you read *The Adventures of Tom Sawyer*, Father Lou?"

"It was one of my favorites as a boy. I read my copy until it fell apart."

"Tom's got something to show you."

Tom's face reddened. "It don't matter."

"No. Go on." Ophelia hoped to teach Tom a lesson about cheating, honesty, and general deception.

"It's just these stupid old things." Tom slowly pulled a handful of tickets from his pocket and held them out to the priest.

Father Lou's eyes met Ophelia's then returned to Tom's face. "How many verses do these count for?"

"At least a hundred, I reckon." Tom's feet suddenly seemed very interesting to him.

"Do you want the Bible or just to be the winner?"

"The winner," said Tom.

Father Lou knelt in front of Tom. "You took a lot of trouble to be the winner."

"I reckon so."

"Do you feel like a winner, Tom?"

"No, sir. I sure don't." He cocked his head. "You're a heap nicer 'n the preacher back home, you know that?"

Father Lou laughed and stood up. "In any case—" he reached behind him to a table covered with Bibles and hymnbooks. He slid a Bible off the stack and placed it in Tom's hands "—some things should just be free. Take it and keep your tickets. Now let's go eat. Do you like roast beef?"

"Yes indeed, sir."

"Then follow me."

Ophelia plodded several steps behind the rest of them to the manse (a house provided by the church for their clergy). She felt ashamed of herself. Intent on teaching Tom a lesson, she'd forgotten what it meant to be kind.

nine

Some People Still Set Foot in Libraries

or You Can't Find Everything on the Internet, Though Some Might Beg to Differ

I love a good library, don't you? There's nothing quite like stacks and stacks of shelves surrounding you while everyone else keeps quiet. With a bottle of hand sanitizer handy, it's possible to while away an entire day without a frenzy of horrible scenarios of pestilence and plague infiltrating one's every thought.

Not only that, but everyone's welcome in the library, one of the few places left that a person can visit voluntarily and feel comfortable. Those coffee shops near the university could learn a thing or two from their public librarian. But then, couldn't we all?

So Ophelia felt contented on that Sunday afternoon while perusing (looking through) volumes she'd located in the Local History section of the old stone building on Cooper Street. She wondered if the tunnels were built for the Underground Railroad, the people in the connected houses providing safe harbor until the escaped slaves, now free men and women, could be conducted further inland to work on farms, or further north for jobs in the mills and factories, and be paid for their services.

But would such a labyrinth of tunnels be necessary? she wondered, flipping through old books with titles such as *Kingscross, a Local History* and *The Founding of Kingscross* and *Kingscross, a Pictorial Retrospective.*

Ophelia lingered with that last one, leafing slowly through the pages as Kingscross, via portraits, drawings, woodcuts, and photographs, transformed from a country village into a thriving university township.

She spotted portraits of Madrigal Pierce's family, noting the strong resemblance that Madrigal still bore to her ancestors. The two pages dedicated to the family spoke volumes. They arrived from England in the early 1700s having been given a land grant by the King of England. (A royal land grant is a big deal and normally includes more acreage than even the wealthiest of people own nowadays.)

So all that's left is the school? Ophelia asked herself. How does a family descend from such vast wealth to Madge desperately trying to maintain the family townhome and keep the school afloat?

One portrait among all the others trapped her gaze. An Aloysius Pierce looked out from the page and across a hundred years, right into Ophelia's eyes. Something about him disquieted her soul. In other words, he made her feel funny inside, like when you know something isn't as it should be, but you can't ascertain (figure out) why. Or you do know why, you just don't understand, nor do you wish to.

Was he a bad man? Was he just sad? Was he in trouble?

She searched through the computer catalogue for all available references concerning the man, but it only yielded the book she had already viewed in an off-hand passage in *Kingscross across the Centuries:*

Aloysius Pierce, creating perhaps the greatest mystery of the family and certainly Kingscross at that time, disappeared on January 29, 1911. What happened to him has never been determined.

That was all. She could find nothing else. Apparently a visit to Madge was in order.

Ophelia gathered up her determination and her notes and hurried back to Rickshaw Street to interview Madrigal Pierce. Surely if anybody knew anything about the Pierce family history and its unsolved mystery, it would be the only one who seemed to care.

Linus, in the meantime, returned to the attic hoping that Cato Grubbs had responded to his communiqué. Indeed, he had. Cato is very diligent about that sort of thing.

Dear Cousin,
Why would I take everyday items from Kingscross? Unless, of course, they originally came from Book World. That could be a possibility, could it not? You don't think the enchanted circle was first discovered by yours truly, do you?

Linus had thought precisely that, actually. Hmm. Poor assumption, he realized.

By the by, young cousin. What possessed your sister to bring Tom Sawyer through? I could go back and filch the treasure, but that seems like stealing candy from a baby. Do me a favor next time and consider my business when you make these decisions. We might arrange a small finder's fee from the proceeds. It takes money to run a lab like ours, and don't forget it.

Your cousin,
Cato Grubbs

Cato had created quite a market for the objects he pilfered from Book World. Who was buying them, the trio didn't know; but the man took his venture seriously. While Linus tried to perfect the formula for bringing over material goods and keeping them from disappearing, Cato Grubbs, in his fancy ruffled shirts and brightly colored vests, traipsed through the pages of literature gathering all manner of valuables.

Linus hit his head with the heel of his hand. "Idiot!"

If Cato Grubbs had to travel into Book World himself to bring back objects, intact and permanent, it was because he'd never discovered the formula that Linus was seeking!

Linus realized he had two choices: continue on as before, realizing that he was breaking new ground, or figure out Cato's secret for traveling through the acids between the worlds at will.

"What is it?" asked Clarice, working on her geometry homework.

Linus explained his conundrum (puzzle) to her.

"Do you have to choose? Why not do both?" she asked.

Linus grinned. She returned the favor.

My dears, when you find someone who believes in you that much, do your best to hold on to them, for they are rare indeed.

When Walter returned from his run, having left Tom with Kylc over at The Pierce School, Linus filled him in.

"It's a bit of a disappointment," said Walter, "that he hasn't yet brought over someone to make things difficult. That Joe character sounds like he could stir things up a bit."

"Thanks, Walt. Cato heard that. You know he did," Linus said.

Walter laughed. "Let's hope so. I'm ready for things to heat up."

Upon further thought, Linus agreed.

Madrigal's dark eyes snapped at Ophelia. "Why do you want to know?"

Oh dear. Poor Ophelia. She hadn't foreseen this. Her brain flipped through a card file of possible explanations, none of which included the fact that she'd disobeyed school policy and gone down into the tunnel.

She plucked one out. And she would follow through with it, she promised herself, to keep it from being a falsehood. "The essay contest that the Founding Daughters of Kingscross is holding. I thought it would be interesting for a Pierce School student to write about the Pierce family."

They sat in Madrigal's private office. While the rest of the rooms of the school were furnished with dark, heavy pieces of furniture (think dark wood carved with fruit, flowers, and curlicues) that had been in her family for much too long, Madrigal's office was bursting with sunlight. It was furnished with modern, smooth furniture made of blond wood, and it included a comfy window seat and two yellow chairs that resembled swans. The white walls were decorated with abstract artwork, erupting with color. This was the headmistress's sanctuary, and she allowed only Ophelia to come inside. Evidently Ms. Pierce needed a confidante (a woman to whom secrets are confided), and she'd picked Ophelia.

Ophelia sipped her tea. Madrigal followed suit. Her expression softened. "Well, that's a fine idea, Ophelia." She laid aside her cup, proving once again that she was a human being like the rest of us. She cleared her throat. "You know, the school is in trouble financially."

"Yes, ma'am. Everyone does."

"I figured as much. I've been trying to get some of the townspeople on board. It's been rough going."

Ophelia couldn't begin to imagine this proud woman asking for money. It must be killing her.

"Perhaps," Madrigal continued, lacing her fingers together, "this essay coming before the Daughters will help them to remember us down here."

"I'll do my best."

"Oh, of course. I wouldn't expect any less of you, Ophelia."

"Are you a Daughter of Kingscross?" she asked.

"Officially, yes. I haven't had time to get involved for years now. All right, if I tell you the family lore about Aloysius, will you promise not to include him in your paper?"

"Yes, ma'am."

"Good, then. Another cup of tea?"

"Please."

ten

Why Is It That the Shadiest of Tales Are Also the Most Interesting?

or Too Bad Birdwistell Wasn't the One Who Disappeared. (Did I Just Say That?)

I did it again, dear reader! I employ the literary device known as a hook *in each book. A hook, if you recall, leaves the reader hanging with the promise of exciting information in the beginning of the next chapter. Writers use this to keep the reader turning pages. Did it work? I dearly hope so. If not, don't blame me. I gave it my best shot.*

The story of Aloysius Pierce as told by Madrigal Pierce to Ophelia, and as Ophelia related it to the three lads, goes like this.

Aloysius came to adulthood at the turn of the century. For us older folks, that means when the 1800s ended and the 1900s began.

He had always been an upstart, falling in with the Mac-Beth brothers. The MacBeths, a loud, hard-drinking lot from Kentucky, made all of their money in gun manufacturing and moonshine. They liked to gamble, being extremely good at it, and they were unafraid to extract the payment of others' gambling debts through, let us just say, extraordinary measures. *(Ask your parents to explain what that means. I simply don't possess the stomach for that sort of thing.)*

As fate would have it, Randolph Pierce, Aloysius's father, passed away leaving his son, and the sole heir, the family fortune. After that, Aloysius's gambling escalated, providing opportunity for more losses.

Aloysius was now married to Penelope Granville—a beautiful woman from another old family in Kingscross and the daughter of the mayor. And he did all he could to keep up appearances. Bit by bit he sold off the family acreage until only the five acres on which the grand country house rested remained of the royal land grant. The couple moved to town permanently under the auspices (pretense) that Penelope, pregnant with their first child, was lonely out in the country and longed to be near her family.

Still he gambled.

Eventually the country house was sold as well.

And still he gambled.

He sold as many of the family valuables as possible until Penelope, now a mother concerned for her children's future, threatened to leave him if he didn't stop.

As you might well guess, Aloysius couldn't stop. Gambling can be an addiction as strong as any drug, drink, chocolate bar, or video game, for that matter.

One day, Aloysius happened upon the tunnel in the basement of the townhouse. He'd been removing an old wardrobe—to sell, no doubt—thereby exposing the entrance. He told no one and returned the wardrobe to its place.

Soon, he knew those tunnels like he knew his own name. *(Nobody knows why they were carved in the first place, but Ophelia is determined to find out!)* And he realized that the arms of the tunnels led to various houses around Kingscross. Items of great value began disappearing around town.

Aloysius failed to return home one evening. And the next. And the evening after that. Penelope, who told no one about her husband's gambling, assumed he had been killed by someone connected to the MacBeths. But she remained silent as to her suspicions. She maintained that silence until Madrigal found Penelope's diary in an old trunk in the attic.

Ophelia finished up the tale. "Penelope walled up the tunnel soon after her husband was declared legally dead. The man who did it had served the family faithfully for years and never told a soul."

"So he was stealing valuables from the houses at the ends of the side corridors," surmised Walter.

"Sounds right," said Linus, lightly tossing a jar labeled Asteroid Dust from hand to hand.

Tom jumped up from the sofa. "See? Pirates wasn't as far off as you thought."

"You're right," said Ophelia, still feeling bad about those tickets. She wouldn't have corrected Tom now even if Aloysius Pierce were to appear and offer her all of the money he'd lost if she'd do just that.

"Then we have to find out where the side tunnels lead," said Walter, dropping to the floor for some push-ups.

"After dinner?" asked Linus. He needed to record a new idea concerning his "plane for all mankind" before his brain filed it too deeply for an easy recovery.

Everyone agreed.

Birdwistell.

Just perfect, thought Ophelia as she walked into the bookshop.

She'd seen the curmudgeonly man more times in the past few days than she had since she and Linus had arrived in Kingscross.

"Come and sit down, dear!" Aunt Portia chimed from where she sat at a large library table blackened by time *(and customers' grimy hands; I don't wish to be unkind, but no amount of hand sanitizer can deal with* that, *dear reader)*. Birdwistell perched opposite her.

"What are you two working on?" Ophelia asked.

"We *two*—" Birdwistell sniffed "—are looking over the lists made out by the burglar's victims."

"What did you have stolen?" Ophelia asked Birdwistell, as she sat next to her aunt. She bit down on an apple that Ronda and Father Lou had left with the family after the party.

Birdwistell winced and sniffed at the same time. "Nothing. Just seeking to be a concerned, helpful member of society," he said.

"Isn't that nice?" asked Aunt Portia with delight.

A little too nice, *if you ask me*, thought Ophelia.

"Ronda told me she had some family jewelry stolen the night of the party, dear," Aunt Portia said. "We have to find this person. And soon!"

"I agree." Ophelia shot a glance at the professor then rose to go find the others.

"Did you find out anything about Aloysius Pierce, dear?" Aunt Portia called out as Ophelia started up the stairs.

"Oh yes!" answered Ophelia.

"Such as?" Birdwistell sat up even straighter. His tone held something she'd never heard in it before. It quivered, just a bit, but with what? Panic? Nerves? Surely it couldn't be that.

"He was quite the gambler," she said.

"Oh. *That.*"

"And quite the thief too!" With that she ran up the stairs and into the kitchen where Linus was pulling down a box of butter cookies.

"Milk all around!" she cried.

Everyone cheered. And not because of the milk, but because it seemed as if that bossy, know-it-all side of Ophelia had disappeared along with Aloysius Pierce.

Thankfully, Aunt Portia tossed the idea of a dinner theme that evening. She sunk four slices of bread into the stainless steel toaster, a bulbous appliance from the 1950s that still, miraculously, toasted. "After that delicious dinner at Father Lou's, I couldn't eat a big supper if I tried!"

The young people issued no complaints, as the memory of Aunt Portia's infamous "brown meal" wasn't buried too deeply. *(I'll leave you to imagine it on your own.)*

"All right," said Ophelia, munching on a tuna salad sandwich. "Let's talk tunnels."

Worry not. Aunt Portia and Uncle Augustus had retired to the living room to eat their sandwiches on TV trays while watching reruns of old BBC sitcoms.

"Should we split up this time?" asked Tom. He'd never eaten canned tuna, and as you might imagine, he scraped it onto the plate and ate the plain toast. The potato chips, on the other hand, delighted him as much as a can of fresh night crawlers and a fishing pole.

"Yep," said Linus. "You and me, Tom?"

"That's good." He placed a stack of five or so chips on his tongue and crunched down.

Ophelia slid a glance at Walter and instantly blushed. *Poor dear, she tried not to. But if she got lost in those tunnels, Walter would be her first choice for a partner.*

"Brilliant," said Walter. "How will we get in the basement with no one the wiser?"

"There's a boarding student life meeting tonight," said Ophelia. "Will Madge notice if you aren't there?"

"I'll figure it out."

"Okay. Meet us at the tunnel entrance in thirty minutes." Walter gave a salute.

"Still got those energy bars?" she asked.

"Oh . . . no. I got a bit hungry last night."

"It's okay," she said. "Just bring water. That should be fine."

A giant clap of thunder jolted the group.

"Whoa!" said Linus.

A firm rain beat at the kitchen windows.

"Won't affect us," Walter said, standing up. "See you in half an hour. We should be able to make quick work of it."

Oh, Walter, Walter, Walter. How could you be so abysmally wrong?

eleven

Some People Just Make Trouble Naturally (Hopefully You Aren't One of Them)

or If You Are a Troublemaker, Don't Come Crying to Me When You Are Friendless and Penniless

$\mathcal{W}$hen Linus entered the attic to collect the flashlights, he knew immediately that something was amiss (not quite right). Some people take little note of their surroundings. In other words, you could rearrange their furniture and they'd barely notice. Other folks? Well, don't help yourself to so much as a Kleenex or they'll have your head. *(The expression "have your head" comes from the days when kings or queens—tyrannical ones, normally—chopped off a person's head for the least little thing.)*

Linus noticed everything. But as long as his experiments remained untouched, he didn't care if the side table sat in the middle of the floor or if the floor lamp sat on the side table. Though Linus was a nice enough person, neither Ophelia nor Walter would even contemplate touching his work. Everyone has their limits. And so they should.

He examined his lab table.

First of all, the levels of the powders in the jars labeled A, B, and C were noticeably diminished. This angered Linus considerably as these powders were quite integral to most of the formulas in Cato Grubbs's notes. He had no idea where the powders came from or how he might renew the supply once it was depleted (used up).

Second, the afghan was no longer draped haphazardly over the arm of the sofa where Ophelia usually cast it when she was finished using it. It was lying on the wooden floor, its creases and folds flowing toward the door as if it had been brushed off by someone on his or her way to the attic steps.

And finally, a piece of Linus's sour apple hard candy, necessary for serious pondering and complex calculations, was missing.

Cato Grubbs! Most assuredly he was the one responsible.

Linus reasoned that if Cato wasn't worried about getting the treasure in *The Adventures of Tom Sawyer*, then he'd decided that serving the teenaged trio a bowlful of bother was a suitable substitute. *(Alliteration strikes again!)*

"That'll teach you, children," echoed in Linus's brain. Yes. Cato Grubbs would delight in teaching them a lesson or two about meddling with the enchanted circle.

But what was he doing in the attic—other than swiping supplies? *(Never mind the fact that Cato owned those three powders and everything else they'd found in the attic lab. But let's not split hairs here.)*

Why did Cato need the powders? Couldn't he go from Book World to Real World at will?

"Or was he bluffing?" Linus mumbled.

"Ready, Linus?" Ophelia called up the steps.

Linus gathered the flashlights and quit the attic.

Walter watched as Linus and Tom walked away, and the pair soon turned into a bobbling light in the darkness.

He turned and gave Ophelia a courtly bow. "Shall we?"

"Certainly, sir."

They ambled along, discussing their theories regarding the possible origin of the tunnels. *(None of them, quite frankly, are worth wasting good ink to record here.)*

Walter stopped. "Do you feel that, O. J.?"

"Feel what?"

He listened again. "Maybe it was nothing. I have a bad feeling about this. I dunno."

Dread squeezed Ophelia's stomach. They had all learned to trust Walter's intuition. "Do you think we should be down here?"

"Don't know that either. Let's just finish as quickly as we can and get out."

Ophelia pulled a long measuring tape out of her pocket. They had decided to measure the space between tunnels, hoping to zero in on which houses in Kingscross had basement openings. "Well, we're charting new territory at any rate," she said.

"Right," said Walter. "And our theory might be rubbish. These tunnels probably have nothing to do with the burglaries. Chances are, most of the entrances are in much the same state as the entrance at school."

"It's true." Ophelia had that exact thought earlier in the day. She just didn't want to voice it until further exploration proved it out. Or not.

Thirty-four feet from the school's tunnel, the first perpendicular passage appeared to their right. They turned and progressed almost fifty feet.

"Does it seem to you," Ophelia asked, jotting down the measurements in a small notepad, "that we're going along Rickshaw Street?"

"Yeah."

"I wonder . . ."

"If this is Seven Hills?" he asked.

Ten feet further down, an oak door with heavy, black iron hardware more suited to a dungeon barred their way.

Ophelia turned the knob and the door swung open with a groan. (Nothing a little WD-40 couldn't put to rights if someone had merely taken the time.) A rectangle of darkness confronted them, and she pierced it with her flashlight.

"Oh my!" she whispered, shining the beam around the space.

Walter stepped inside what appeared to be a storage room. Bottles of liquids and jars of powders and shriveled items (mostly unrecognizable, save for an old potato) were stuffed onto the shelves of a bookcase like the ones in Aunt Portia's shop.

Walter whistled. "Linus will be happy to see this."

"No kidding." Ophelia joined him in the room and continued circling the space with her flashlight. She stopped when her beam landed on a clump of fabric, yellowed and dirty. (The kindest way to describe it would be "once white.") She approached where the fabric hung limply on a faded pink satin hanger on the back of a door. Pulling the fabric toward her, Ophelia noticed buttons and lace, a sleeve with a black cuff, and the neckline was black too. "This looks like an old wedding gown," she said.

The dress seemed stitched with hope and frayed by despair. For a reason she couldn't describe, it saddened Ophelia's heart.

A veil peeked out from behind the dress. Ophelia tried to pull it out to get a better look, but her fingers punctured the fabric and disintegrated the netting on contact. "Dry rot," she said.

"Do you know whose dress it could be?" asked Walter.

Ophelia couldn't imagine. She just hoped it wasn't the wedding gown from some folk tale where the girl is found in the trunk years after she disappeared on her wedding day. Imagine a hapless (deserving of pity) young bride, so full of hope and bursting with so much love, locked in a trunk. Yet no one hears her cries or the pummeling of her fists against the inside of the trunk lid.

Really?

I hope you'll allow me to interject an aside here, since Walter and Ophelia are perfectly safe in the basement of the Seven Hills bookshop. (I'm not interrupting a sword fight, after all.)

By the way, an aside usually has nothing to do with the movement of the story, but hopefully it proves interesting to the reader. In this case, I do hope you are interested in becoming a halfway decent writer. Something important to consider at the very start of your story is believability. Now, the enchanted circle might not be believable to you there in your boring, run-of-the-mill world. But you've cheerfully suspended your disbelief and have allowed me to write about something fantastical.

However, if in the middle of this very chapter I were to write that Ophelia grew wings, Linus woke up with a gaze that could set fire to anything except the pair of spectacles (glasses) on his face, and Walter had titanium claws three times the size of his hands that could shoot out from the backs of his hands (but didn't impede his wrist movements whatsoever), then you'd think, "Well, that sure came out of nowhere."

Not to mention that I would be pilfering someone else's ideas.

What does all of this have to do with Walter and Ophelia in the storage room? Only that if you should ever read that folk tale about the bride locked in the trunk (after your feelings of sadness for the young bride have settled down, of course), you'll probably ask yourself:

How in the world did her family not find her? She was still in the house, wasn't she? They set up a search party. Why wouldn't they have found her eventually? And how did an adult fall completely, legs and all, into a trunk, and then allow the lid to latch when clearly her arm would have easily been able to stop it?

The author of this short story never once told us that the bride possessed the coordination of a pair of old slippers (and I'm just putting two and two together here, folks).

In other words, dear reader, it never hurts to analyze a story so you don't make the same mistakes in your own writings. Don't bother to do that with this book, however. It would waste your time and, as the saying goes, serve as an exercise in futility to seek out such gross errors among its pages. If you don't like it, take it up with the Queen of England. She is only a figurehead monarch, after all, and she might be glad for something to do.

Ophelia let the moldering garments fall back into place against the door. "This must be the door to the bookshop." She rooted around for the doorknob and gripped it. The doorknob turned easily, allowing them to enter another room. However, this one was not a rectangle of darkness. An anemic (in this case, weak, not very bright) light emanated from a bare bulb in the ceiling.

The walls were fashioned from the same stone blocks as the basement of the house on Rickshaw Street, and the cramped space easily displayed its spare contents: a chest of drawers carved with two great dragons and the moon, an open sea captain's trunk foaming with ruffled men's clothing, a collection of ornamented walking sticks and canes in an umbrella stand in the corner. And all of it pointed to Cato Grubbs.

A cot draped with a fringed crimson throw rounded out the eclectic (selected from various sources) mix of furniture, and it was presently occupied.

Ophelia immediately recognized the dozing man by his caramel complexion, his proud brow and head of heavy hair, black as a panther's. "It's Injun Joe," she whispered in Walter's ear.

"Are you sure?"

"Who else could it be? I mean, considering that the book he's from is open right now."

They backed out of the room, silently shutting the door behind them and then retreated to the tunnel.

"I do hope we didn't leave behind any mark of our presence," said Walter, as he screwed off the top of his water bottle and passed it to Ophelia.

She took a large gulp. The sight of Joe had dried up her throat almost instantly.

Walter followed suit, taking several mouthfuls. *(He was obviously unconcerned about sharing someone else's germs. Nobody said he was perfect.)* "I think we found out who's using the tunnels," he said.

"Cato Grubbs. It's how he moves the literary objects out, I suppose."

"Right."

They abandoned any further mapping of the tunnels to go find Linus and Tom.

After fifteen minutes, the beams of their flashlights melded together between the four of them.

"All doors locked so far," said Linus.

"One we couldn't even get to!" Tom said. "There was a cave-in!"

"Wow," Ophelia said as she leaned against the tunnel wall for strength. "You guys are never going to believe what we found."

Ophelia felt this adventure slipping by more quickly than any of the others. She had yet to address Joe's awful fate with Tom, and now the violent man was asleep in their basement.

The clock in the attic chimed nine. Only fourteen hours remained until Tom's return to St. Petersburg, and they hadn't even figured out who was stealing the antiques.

They lounged around the attic. Tom, using Linus's utility knife, whittled away at a stick he'd found in the park earlier. Walter did push-ups and knee bends. Ophelia found a piece of string on the sofa and was twisting it between her fingers. Linus concentrated on a drawing.

"So Cato's living here," Linus said, not looking up from his task.

"Seems to be the case," said Walter.

"He's so wily," said Ophelia. She picked up the afghan off the floor and spread it across her lap. "He pocketed the money from the sale of this building to Aunt Portia and Uncle Augustus, and he still lives here."

"Smart," said Linus.

"What does he need all of this money for anyway?" asked Walter.

The twins shrugged. Who knew?

"What about Injun Joe?" asked Tom, his fear of the man propelling the words forward at breakneck speed.

"Why are you so frightened of him, mate?" asked Walter.

The rain outside pelted the trefoil window.

"He wants to kill me," said Tom.

A bolt of lightning struck nearby, crackling their eardrums as a blinding white light flashed outside the window.

All went dark.

twelve

Cato Grubbs Goes Too Far

or Be Careful When You Try to Teach Someone a Lesson.
Your Regret Could Easily Outweigh Their Learning
Experience. Then Again, You Might Have No Regrets at All.

Ophelia! Linus!" Aunt Portia called up the attic staircase. "Are you children all right?"

Ophelia ran to the steps. "We're fine," she whispered. So far Uncle Augustus didn't know about the attic, and they wanted to keep it that way.

"What about Tom?" Aunt Portia seemed to be only a voice in the dark stairwell.

"I ain't skeered!" shouted Tom.

Ophelia winced and cast a "Shh!" in his general direction. "Where's Uncle Auggie?"

"He decided to go play cribbage. Don't worry, dear. Your secret is still safe."

"Everything all right downstairs?"

"On this floor, dear. I'm just about to check on the shop."

"No!" Ophelia cried. "Umm, what I mean is, let us do that for you."

"Whyever is that nec—"

Walter suddenly appeared next to Ophelia, holding the flashlight. "Just trying to do our bit, Aunt Portia."

She clapped her hands. "Well, aren't you delightful! Please, go ahead then. I'm just as happy to return to bed." She backed out of the stairwell and closed the door behind her.

Ophelia puffed out a sigh of relief.

Linus stood up as Tom climbed to his feet, laying his knife and wooden stick on the table under the window.

"Let's go," said Walter.

The shop was dimly illuminated by a battery-powered night-light near the section labeled BRITISH POETRY, 1800–1875.

They circled their flashlights around the room.

"Let's see if we can find the door to Cato's room," said Ophelia.

They all tromped down into the dark basement, the briny smell of the floodwaters that had filled this room in July still saturated the air. Talk about a swimming pool! Everything had been removed and most everything discarded. It was just a bunch of Cato's old junk anyway.

"It shouldn't be too hard to find," said Ophelia.

Oh, Ophelia!

They carefully ran their lights along the masonry (stone-work), hunting for irregularities in the mortar connecting one stone to another. They even pressed on the stones, hoping to find a spring-loaded device that might expose a hidden door. *(Perhaps that only happens in the movies where nothing is too much trouble.)*

No luck.

"Cato must go in and out through the tunnels," Walter said. "There's nothing here."

"Or he's hidden the entrance beyond our ability to find it," said Ophelia.

Linus didn't doubt that for a second.

"Well, at least Joe can't get in the house," said Ophelia. "So things are looking up, right?"

Allow me a bit of foreshadowing here, dear reader. Maybe you'll realize later on in the story what I was referring to. Or maybe not.

Imagine Tom's feelings about now. Imagine finding out that the man who knows you testified against him in a court of law for a murder he committed out of greed and revenge—a man you thought was dead and would trouble you no longer—breathes once again and is sleeping in a secret basement room in the very house in which you are staying.

"Are you sure I can't go back through that circle now?" Tom asked, picking up his whittling.

"Unfortunately, yes," said Linus.

Ophelia felt sick. If anything happened to Tom . . . "Cato could take you back, but I don't see that happening."

"Maybe you had better tell us more about Joe," Walter suggested.

"Well," Tom hesitated.

"Would you like me to tell them?" Ophelia asked in a gentle voice.

Tom nodded. "I'd be obliged."

"One night," she began, "Tom and Huck went to the graveyard to get rid of some warts with a dead cat that Huck bought off a boy for a blue ticket and a bladder he got at the slaughterhouse."

Tom stared openmouthed at Ophelia. "Why, you really *do* know where I been and what I done!"

"Uh-huh. Anyway, they were waiting to do their thing over a freshly dug grave when three men appeared."

"Hold up." Linus raised a hand. "A dead cat cures warts?"

"Sure does," said Tom. "But not as good as stumpwater and eleven steps after midnight."

"Folk remedies," said Ophelia, casting a glance in her brother's direction to silently inform him that this was neither the time nor the place for a lesson about how a virus, not a frog, brings on warts.

"Okay." Linus shrugged.

"Apparently, one of the three men had snubbed Joe—"

"Not Joe Harper, Ophelia. Injun Joe," said Tom.

Oh dear, she thought. "We don't use words like *injun* anymore."

"Whyever not?"

"Would you like being described as 'White Tom' all of your life?"

Tom laughed and laughed. "Why would anybody want to call me that?"

"We just try to be a little more respectful nowadays, give people a chance to be who they are without attaching other names to them that they weren't born with, especially names that might cause others to view them suspiciously—even if they've never done anything to hurt anybody."

"But Injun Joe is a thief, a liar, and a murderer. And he's a drunk to boot!"

"Anybody can be those things, mate, no matter what the color of their skin might be," said Walter.

"But what does callin' him 'Injun Joe' have to do with—"

"Nevermind!" cried Ophelia. "We'll just call him 'Joe' from now on, all right?"

"I s'pose," said Tom.

Trying to explain twenty-first–century politics to a boy

who lived that many years ago would take much longer than five minutes. Ophelia could only hope she'd given Tom something to think about.

She continued the tale. "Doc Robinson wanted to exhume (dig up) a man's body, and he'd paid Joe and a man named Muff Potter an agreed upon amount to do the digging. After the body was raised, Joe demanded more money for the job. You see, he was seeking revenge for being poorly treated by Doc Robinson five years earlier. When Joe had asked the doctor for a handout (money or food given to a needy person), Doc Robinson had turned him away without a dime. So after the doctor refused to pay Joe and Muff more for their digging work, a fight broke out. In the end Joe stabbed Doc Robinson in the chest and killed him."

"But Muff Potter got knocked out cold by Doc Robinson afore then!" Tom supplied. "So Joe blamed it all on Muff."

"Right," said Ophelia. "And Muff had been so drunk at the time, he figured that because he'd woken up with the murder weapon in his hand—where Joe put it—it must be true."

"So they threwed *Muff* in jail instead," said Tom. "Huck and I were mighty afeard to tell the truth of it all, but we tried to do right by old Muff. We tried to make his stay a mite easier."

"It's true," said Ophelia. "Well, the truth finally came out because Tom was brave enough to tell it. Joe was convicted and sentenced to hang, but he escaped. He left the area for a while too. But now the problem is that we don't know from which spot in the book Cato yanked him over to Real World."

"It might have been *before* the murder?" Tom asked, with hope shining in his eyes.

Ophelia nodded.

"We have to find that out," said Walter. "It will make all the difference."

"On it," said Linus, swiveling on his stool toward his worktable. He slid the notebook toward him and grabbed a pencil.

Dear Cousin Cato,

We found Joe. Care to tell us if you brought him over pre- or post-murder?

Tom's just a little boy.

Thank you.

Your Cousin,

Linus Easterday

He turned back to the group. "What now?"

The clock chimed ten. The lights flickered back on.

"I'd better get back," said Walter, "before Madge discovers I'm missing."

After he left, Ophelia picked up her worrying string once more and began fidgeting with it. "Maybe we should work on finding the burglar. There's nothing we can do about Joe for now."

"We could do homework," said Linus.

They looked at each other, hesitated, then said in unison, "Nah!"

"How about it, Tom?" Ophelia asked. "Want to help us solve the mystery?"

"Does it include buried treasure?" he asked.

Ophelia remembered the empty shelves in the cave by the river. "It just might."

thirteen

To Catch a Thief

or Why Do People Like Dirty Old Things Anyway?

*L*inus never trusted antiques. Consider that blue sofa in the attic. Ophelia and Walter heedlessly flopped all of their weight on the old piece, trusting—like motorists driving across a bridge about which they know positively nothing—that those one-hundred-year-old legs will support them. His parents, the lepidopterologists (entomologists who specialize in the collection and study of butterflies and moths), adored old stuff—particularly creepy portraits of long-dead people whom none of them knew.

Dr. Julia Easterday would come home with a new one at least once a month, claiming she pitied the poor man or woman trapped, unloved, inside some store and not living in a proper home. *(Oh, the irony!)* Ophelia, on the other hand, fabricated (made up) fanciful stories about not only the stoic faces staring down at them from the walls, but the furniture, the candlesticks, even the antique linens that had been handed down on the Easterday side of the family for generations.

"I just think they smell funny," Linus always said.

The lad and I agree about that. And imagine the decades

of germs built up on that fabric. Heavens, it's almost too overwhelming to contemplate. Linus, however, was not worried about germs and dirt, as his mountainous pile of dirty laundry would attest. It sat on the floor next to the beanbag chair that both Tom and Ophelia refused to sit on. Talk about something smelling funny.

Linus, Tom, and Ophelia were now gathered in Linus's bedroom. At Ophelia's suggestion that they find a link between the stolen items, Linus opened a search engine on his desktop computer.

"Two Louis the Fourteenth side chairs," said Ophelia, reading down the list that Father Lou had distributed to the community group. "A Napoleon era sideboard. A Fabergé egg." She looked up. "Wow. I'd like to have seen that for myself."

Fabergé *eggs, dear readers, fashioned of gold and precious gems by a man named Carl Fabergé, are some of the most delightful pieces an eye will ever behold. Tsar Nicholas of Russia owned several. (Not that they did him any good in the end, but never mind about that.) Look them up! You'll be glad you did.*

"Hey," said Ophelia. "Look at Aunt Portia's list! The books are by Dumas, Hugo, Pascale, and Descartes."

"They're all French authors," said Linus.

"French antiques." Ophelia jotted that note next to the list of stolen goods. "What about Ronda's missing jewelry?"

"We could ask her," said Linus.

"Okay. I guess that's not all that important. What's important is that we've got a French connection going here."

Ophelia had no idea that she'd just referred to a movie

from the '70s. The child watches little television, bless her soul.

We should see if there are any similarities between the victims, Linus thought.

"What about the people whose things were burgled?" asked Ophelia.

The three of them sat in a circle on the floor with the list in the middle of them.

"I don't know them folks," said Tom. "Sorry."

"Let's see." Ophelia ran her index finger down the list. "I don't know all of them, but it seems like an awful lot of them work at the University."

Linus scanned the list. "Except for Aunt Portia and Ronda."

Now you might be wondering whether Portia and Ronda were in cahoots with one another, donning black clothing and skulking about town in the dark early morning hours, with sacks in hand, purloining (stealing) French loot from the pleasant, unsuspecting citizens of Kingscross.

Don't worry. I wasn't either.

"Now let's go through everyone's guest list by alphabet," suggested Ophelia.

"A, B, C, D, E . . . " Tom recited.

Ophelia, not wishing to correct him again, let him get all the way to Z. "Excellent. Now let's find all of the names beginning with A on these lists."

Anderson, Angelo, Appmann, Azalea.

"Azalea?" said Linus.

"How pretty!" exclaimed Ophelia.

Linus and Tom exchanged you've-got-to-be-kidding-me glances. They burst out laughing.

"What?" asked Ophelia.

"Azalea? Really?" Linus laughed again.

"Whatever." She returned to the lists. "None of the A names are found on all of the guest lists."

"How about them Bs?" Tom reached for an apple from the bowl that Ophelia had brought upstairs for the occasion.

"All right. Let's see."

Tom bit down with a great crunching snap. A brief puff of fresh apple cider scent hovered between the three. Linus reached for an apple too.

"Baker, Bandolino . . ." Ophelia slid her finger down the rosters. "Oh. Wow."

"What?" Linus leaned over the paper.

"Birdwistell. At every single event."

Linus raised his eyebrows.

"What's a bird's whistle got to do with this here?" asked Tom.

"Not a what," replied Ophelia, "but a *who*."

"Professor Kelvin Birdwistell," Linus supplied.

"Who's that?"

Ophelia huffed. "Only the meanest, most prideful man that's ever come to this house."

"Meaner than Injun Joe?"

"I don't think he's murdered anyone, if that's what you mean, Tom."

"Well, that's good." Satisfied, Tom leaned back against Linus's bed.

How's that for perspective?

"Maybe we should check the rest of the names, you know, just to make sure he's not the only one," she said.

For the next fifteen minutes, she made her way through

116

the lists of names while Tom threw Linus's baseball in the air, looking as bored as a boy stuck inside a room on a rainy evening should.

"Somebody named Betty Holiday and Frances Clark-Sanderson, she teaches art at the University, are the only other people who attended all of the events." She set the lists aside. "My money's still on Birdwistell."

Linus clacked away on his keyboard. At his old school, he'd been the eighth-grade typing champ, typing ninety-five words per minute without a mistake.

This just goes to show you, young person, that even if you can't play football or ice skate, there may be nothing wrong with your hands. You might be picked last in P.E. class, but that doesn't mean you can't become a great artist or musician someday. So remember that when your classmates make you feel as worthwhile as a bucket with a hole. You can be more than they ever dreamed. Take me, for example, not that my colleagues in the English Department recognize such genius.

"Give me a minute," Linus said. "I'm almost in."

"Are you hacking?" asked Ophelia.

"What's 'hacking'?" Tom got to his feet and stood beside Linus. He'd already been shown the computer, and it seemed like no fun whatsoever to Tom. "Who wants to stay home all the good long day and look at pitchers?" he'd said.

"Birdwistell's email?" Ophelia leaned over and examined the screen. The website banner displayed the words KINGSCROSS UNIVERSITY and the school crest of a pelican, four keys, and a severed head.

FACULTY LOGIN proclaimed the reason for the webpage, and the email address and password boxes shone white.

"The email address is easy enough." Linus typed K.BIRDWISTELL.PHILOSOPHY@KINGSCROSSUNIVERSITY.EDU. "Now for the password."

Asterisks appeared on the screen as he typed. Then he pressed ENTER with his right pinkie. Two seconds later, Professor Birdwistell's emails cascaded down the page arranged by date, listed from today all the way back to December two years ago. The older ones were from his sister, Cecily.

"What was his password?" asked Ophelia.

"Password."

"Are you kidding?"

"It's an age thing," said Linus. His eyes glowed. "Let's look at some mail."

Yes, yes, yes! I know it's against the law! I'm not saying Linus was within his legal rights. I'm simply telling you what happened. If you don't like it, please contact Father Lou Wellborne, All Souls Episcopal Church, 297 Rickshaw Street, Kingscross.

Linus clicked on the oldest email first. "Wow."

Ophelia gasped.

"What?" asked Tom.

Ophelia pointed to the email address: CECILY@BIRDWISTELLANTIQUES.COM.

Linus pulled up another window on the browser and typed in the Web address. Up popped the website for Birdwistell Antiques in Chantilly, Virginia.

SPECIALIZING IN FRENCH ANTIQUES proclaimed the tasteful crimson letters on a cream background. Underneath that, a flashing banner advertised that Birdwistell Antiques was having a liquidation sale.

"Bingo." Linus sat back in his chair.

"Huh?" asked Tom.

"We've got him." Ophelia squeezed Linus's shoulder and turned to Tom. "We found the burglar."

"Looks like he's been trying to keep his sister's business afloat," said Linus.

Ophelia felt sad at that piece of information. But just a little.

Ophelia checked the computer's clock. "Ten forty-five."

"Pretty good," said Linus.

"We made quick work of that, didn't we, Tom?"

"I can't wait to see his face!" Tom said.

"I'll tell Walt." Linus stood and grabbed a hoodie off the bed.

After he left the room, Ophelia turned to Tom. "Are you sleepy?"

"Naw."

"Me neither. There are only about twelve hours until you go back. Anything you want to do?"

"Can we go back downstairs? I reckon I'd like to take a copy of my book back with me. Only this one—" he slid the dog-eared paperback out of his jacket pocket "—might be suspicious looking with this floppy cover. Ours are a lot harder." He handed the book to Ophelia. "I was reading it at the park this morning," he explained.

"Why not?" She put it in her own pocket.

Tom grabbed another apple as they made their way to the door.

Downstairs in the bookshop, the brass chandelier lights with gold linen shades cast a warm glow over the store.

"It's nice here," said Tom. "Your aunt is a kind lady. Everybody's been real nice."

None of the other travelers had been excited about returning to their native world. "Will it be hard to go back?" Ophelia led Tom to the shelves labeled AMERICAN LITERATURE, 1800–1850.

"I miss my friends. I even miss Sid. Well, just a little."

"Aunt Polly and Becky?"

He nodded.

"Well, it won't be long before the circle opens up once more."

She searched the shelves filled with books arranged alphabetically by last name of the author. "Twain, Twain." Her fingertips slid along the names: Hawthorne, Melville, Stowe . . . "Here it is!" Her index finger curled over the top of the book's spine, and she tipped it into her hand.

Tom accepted the hardback book bound in leaf green fabric. "The Adventures of Tom Sawyer," he read aloud, then looked up at Ophelia. "Well, don't this just beat all?"

"It sure does."

"Look here, Ophelia!" He held the book out in front of him with both hands. "Tom Sawyer, that's me, right there on the cover!"

The rain still beat its wet fists against the shop's front windows.

"Want some hot chocolate?" she asked.

"Huh?

"Don't worry. You'll like it."

Near the sales counter, Aunt Portia had installed a hot beverage machine. Cappuccinos, lattes, coffee, and hot chocolate were dispensed at the simple touch of a button.

(*Take* that *you bumptious (self-important) coffee bars! Portia hoped to drum up more business this way because, heaven help us, books aren't enough anymore. Frankly, the coffee tastes much better at Seven Hills than what I get out of the vending machine in the English Department. Maybe it isn't such a bad idea, after all!)*

Ophelia positioned a white paper cup beneath the spout and pressed the backlit green button beside the words HOT COCOA.

As the machine resurrected itself from the sleep of a store closed on Sunday evening *(imagine that!)*, the *pfoof* sound of powder falling and then hot water spluttering hid the sound of the basement door opening. Tom's fascination with this marvel of machinery and Ophelia's feeble explanation of how it worked stole all of their attention.

"Not a sound," a low voice whispered, as its owner snatched Tom from behind just as Ophelia picked up the cup of hot cocoa.

They both shouted in surprise, and Ophelia jumped, sloshing the scalding liquid over her hand. "Ow!"

Joe brandished (shook or waved) a knife. The lights from the chandelier danced along its blade, as his hand comfortably gripping the bone handle. "I said quiet."

"Injun Joe!" cried Tom.

Joe grabbed Tom by his hair.

"Ouch!"

"If you two don't keep still, I'll kill you both right here." Ophelia forgot about her burned hand.

fourteen

A Dark Darker Than Dark
or Who Knew So Much Could Happen Underground?

Cato Grubbs never failed to throw a little extra spice into the stew of trouble he created for the trio around the eleventh of every month. Frollo, the evil alchemist deacon who raised Quasimodo, headed the lineup. Starbuck, though an honorable fellow and first mate aboard Captain Ahab's whaling ship *The Pequod*, sufficiently threw matters off as well. And the three musketeers made for a rousing fight. But all of these people put together weren't as dangerous to Linus, Ophelia, and Walter as Joe was to Tom.

Joe was what was then called a "half-breed." One parent was Native American; the other was Caucasian. Most likely, he wasn't accepted by either society. I tell you this, dear reader, to enable you to look at characters in a more well-rounded manner. While Mark Twain doesn't appear to do the same for Joe, you can know that when a human being is cast to the rim of society through no fault of his own, he most likely will not feel responsible to, or possess even a basic respect for, the people who placed him there.

Bear this in mind. Thank you. And don't forget to brush your teeth before going to bed.

Ophelia, then Tom, climbed down the basement steps into Cato's secret lair.

All right, all right! Lair *might be overstating it somewhat. Villains much more suave and superheroes with superhuman strength have lairs. The Bat Cave would qualify. Cato Grubbs lived in a musty room in the basement of a bookstore, a place that smelled of earth, stone, minerals, mothballs, stale sweat, and empty containers of ramen noodles. The word* pigsty *might be more appropriate.*

~~Joe followed.~~

"Do you know how you got here?" asked Ophelia.

Joe laughed a single "Hunh" though partially closed lips, his dark eyes hard. "Some fancy feller found me in McDougal's Cave. Brought me right here." He glared at Tom. "You know 'bout where he is, boy?"

Tom shook his head like a dog that just climbed out of a lake. "No! No, sir! I ain't never see'd that man!"

"Then why you in the house, Tom Sawyer?"

Ophelia ignored the question. "Did that fancy man tell you Tom would be here?"

"He sure enough did." Joe gripped the knife harder and rested the point beneath Tom's chin. "Now, you gonna get me back to where I can find the treasure, ain't you?"

Ophelia answered, "But we're not—"

"Yes, sir," Tom said. "You just follow me, and we'll find it quicker than a wink, I reckon."

"You'd better."

Joe opened the door to the tunnel and pushed them through. As Joe was closing the door, Tom whispered to Ophelia, "As long as he thinks we know where the treasure is, I reckon he'll keep us alive. Just follow my lead."

This, thought Ophelia, *is one bright little boy.*

And she was exactly right.

The darkness swallowed them whole as the door to the world above closed behind Joe.

A loud click echoed against the stone walls.

Ophelia snapped on her light.

"What's that?" Joe barked.

"It's like a tiny kerosene lamp," she said.

And he was satisfied. "Get going, you," he said, giving Tom a stiff shove.

"Hey!" Tom shouted, put out.

Ophelia stifled a smile. Maybe they would be all right after all.

Linus and Walter crawled through the not-so-secret door in the bathroom from the secret passage to The Pierce School.

They went directly to the attic where they could talk without whispering.

"Should we take this to the police?" asked Linus.

"Too late for that now, mate. We should wait until morning."

Linus reached for his notebook hoping to find a reply from Cato, which he found.

"Oh no," he said.

Walter held out his hand, knowing better than to ask Linus to read it aloud.

Post-murder. Post-trial. Post-escape.
Have fun, little meddlers.

Rage filled Walter's face. He took three deep breaths and fisted his hands into tense balls of bone and tendon.

Linus took back the notebook feeling much the same as Walter, but never one to show the extent of his emotions.

"Okay," said Walter. "This is bloody awful. I was *stupid* enough to think even Grubbs has his limits."

"Me too."

"Birdwistell can wait. We'd better find Ophelia and Tom and figure out what to do with Joe. Hopefully he's still in Cato's quarters."

They checked Ophelia's room first. Laden as it was with books and clothes scattered like a bird lady's breadcrumbs *(at least Linus piles his dirty clothing)*, they lifted her comforter just to make sure she wasn't underneath it.

Linus led the way down the hall to his own room.

"Not here either. Maybe they're having a snack."

Linus pointed to the apple bowl. "Another one is missing, so maybe not."

Walter scratched the back of his neck. "How in the—"

"I notice things. I count things."

"Apparently," Walter mumbled.

Nobody was in the kitchen either. Linus began to worry, but he said nothing other than, "Bookshop."

"Right."

Each footstep down the stairs to Seven Hills Better Books deposited another stone of unease into their stomachs. Walter's intuition raised the hairs on his arms like stalks of grass. He said nothing.

And the boys' silence meant nothing because as soon as they pushed open the door to the shop, the light from the chandelier exposed the spilled cup of hot chocolate. And

126

there at the foot of the basement steps, its hard cover open and lying facedown, lay *The Adventures of Tom Sawyer*.

Linus moved first, running down the basement stairs with more speed and agility than Walter would have imagined him capable.

He descended into the basement to find a set of wooden attic stairs spilling from a hole in the basement ceiling. He scrambled up into the opening, Walter at his heels. Only about two feet of air rested between the floor and ceiling.

"How could this not be noticed upstairs?" Walter whispered when they both lay on their bellies.

"False ceiling." Linus turned on the flashlight that he had forgotten to remove from his hoodie pocket, fortunately. "See?"

The light shone around a space roughly the same footprint as the house.

"Why would anyone build this?"

"Don't know," Linus said. "But there's where it leads."

Another opening with a second set of pull-down stairs, lit up under his flashlight.

"Guess there are more mysteries in this place than just the attic," said Walter. "That must lead to Cato's room."

Linus crawled over and looked down. "Nobody's in there."

"Then let's follow them!"

Linus laid a hand on his friend's arm. "Hold up."

"But, mate. Ophelia and Tom might be—"

"Joe is most likely armed. Let's get Father Lou."

"I see your point." As the one who'd roamed the streets of London with quick fists and a sharp knife, Walter didn't know why he hadn't thought of that himself.

"Let's just hope he isn't asleep," said Linus, following Walter up the basement steps.

They yanked open the front door of the shop and ran across the street, the rain soaking them as thoroughly as a bucket of water thrown over their heads.

A bounty hunter finds people who are wanted by the law. And like a shark fisherman, he or she reels them in for a price. That price is called the *bounty*. Father Lou has never hunted down a roll of power towels. *(Although there's nothing more sanitary than a clean paper towel to clear up a mess.)*

Due to the fact that Father Lou—or as he was known back then, "Lou the Bonecrusher"—handed out violence (punches, kicks, choke holds) like a calling card, he slept, as the saying goes, with one eye open. In other words, he woke at the slightest sound with a glint in his eye, fists curled, ready for a fight.

Please let him be awake, Linus thought. He glanced at his watch when they stopped under the small porch roof that hovered over the landing in front of the dark blue kitchen door.

11:11 P.M.

Maybe that was a good sign.

He lifted a fist to knock, knowing it would vibrate the white cotton curtains behind the door's window, and hoping the dark kitchen didn't mean there was a sleeping priest inside. "Twelve hours to go."

"We've got to find them," said Walter. "I don't think Ophelia would ever forgive herself if Tom was eaten by the acids between the worlds."

"He's just a kid."

Walter sighed. "Yeah. I can't stand Cato."

Linus rapped on the door as loudly as he could.

fifteen

Madge Will Be Madge

or Why Right Now?

Father Lou understood firsthand the dangerous waters in which Tom and Ophelia were now swimming. "A man on the run—and after a murder conviction, too—is one of the most desperate kind." He was thankful he'd discarded all of his guns when he took the collar of a priest. A gun would be far too dangerous in the close, dark tunnels, and fear was the greatest tempter. He opened his nightstand drawer and extricated (took out) his Bowie knife. If a fight ensued, at least it would be fair. Then again, five people were believed to be dead at the man's hands already.

Father Lou's tender heart heavied a little. Could there be some sort of turnaround for Joe here in Real World?

Well, a person can always hope. He pulled on his leather jacket.

He inwardly uttered a quick prayer of protection for all concerned, and requested a miraculous intervention and outcome as well. *Although I'm not trying to be pushy or tell You what to do,* he prayed. Lou slipped the knife into the back pocket of his jeans, then quickly added, *And please make it so that I'm not forced to use this thing. I'd really rather not.*

Father Lou is much smarter than Linus and Walter put together, if one factors in the ability to remember to take along an umbrella when the sky decides to overflow, which I do.

The three men dashed into the bookshop.

Father Lou closed the umbrella and stuffed the dripping, believe it or not, Tweety Bird bumbershoot (a very old-fashioned word for *umbrella*) in a stand by the door. One can assume a younger person left it behind at the church. "Have you said anything to your aunt and uncle, Linus?"

"Uh . . . no."

"I certainly haven't uttered a word to Madge," Walter volunteered.

"I can hardly blame you there." He marched over to the counter. "Let's write a quick note and leave it here, just in case."

Father Lou glanced at his watch. On a piece of scratch paper that Portia kept near the register, he scribbled the words:

> *We've gone into the tunnels at 11:29 P.M. on Sunday the 13th to find Ophelia and Tom whom we suspect are already in there. The tunnels are accessed over at the school.*
>
> *Linus, Walter, and Father Lou*

"Good. We've covered our bases," he said.

Walter stood at the basement steps. "This way, Father."

Several minutes later, they gathered in Cato's secret room. Walter opened the door to the storage area, and the old wedding dress swung with the door. The light bulb still burned like a watching eye from its socket in the ceiling.

"Whoa," said Father Lou, quickly looking around as they passed through. "Look at all this junk."

"Wow," Linus muttered, his eyes taking in the jars and tins of supplies. He was a bit disappointed in himself, considering the circumstances, at the relief he felt when he spied the A, B, and C powders on the uppermost shelf.

"Here's the door to the tunnel." Walter turned the handle and pulled. "Locked? That's odd."

Father Lou tried. "There must be a latch on the other side so Cato can lock himself inside or outside of this dump, whatever he needs."

"That leaves only two ways we know of to enter the tunnels," Walter said, heading back into Cato's room. "Either the cave by the river or the basement of the school."

"The river entrance isn't far from the dam," said Linus.

"With this rain, I don't trust the river," said Father Lou.

"And the school tunnel is quite a bit closer." Walter closed the storage room door behind them.

"Madge," said Linus.

"I'd almost rather brave the river," said Father Lou, as he disappeared into the ceiling.

"I could say amen to that," mumbled Walter, the next one to climb up.

And I could say amen to that amen, thought Linus, following Walter into the darkness.

Thankfully, Aunt Portia and Uncle Augustus were long asleep by the time the three rescuers tiptoed down the hall to the bathroom.

Perhaps *tiptoed* isn't quite right. Father Lou and Linus walked lightly, a gingerly placing of the entire foot on the floor. Walter practiced his T'ai Chi steps, placing his heel first, then rolling to a flat foot. He pivoted the heel as he redistributed his weight. He was silent as a cat and just as graceful.

When they entered the bathroom and Linus knelt to remove the passageway door, Walter couldn't help but wonder what might happen to them all. A fight would probably erupt if Joe was as desperate as Father Lou claimed. Thankfully, Walter knew how to keep his head. But the words of Sensei Yang echoed in his mind as he crawled along the secret passage: *If you use what I have taught you against another human being, it is only because you failed. The real victory is not to fight at all.*

Walter hadn't fully understood that statement until now. When he was a small lad, filled with anger and wanting only to lash out, his mum would take him by the shoulders, look into his eyes, and say, "Use your words, lovey."

The thought of the mum he loved so much made Walter all the more fearful. They only had each other in this world, really. Except for Auntie Max, but she was a downright kook sometimes.

He needed to remember their wisdom just then.

Could they reason with Joe? He hoped so. Perhaps his own desperation to do the right thing, to turn his back on who he had become in London, had grown roots deep enough to match the desperation of the man who had kidnapped the girl Walter admired most.

Oh yeah, and Father Lou accompanied them. *(Sometimes Walter gets a little big for his britches, but it's mostly in his head, so you can forgive him.)*

They resumed their silent stepping out of the supply closet, down the hallway of the boys' dormitory wing, and across the balcony overlooking the grand entry hall.

Thankfully, burgundy carpet runners flowed down the two curved staircases, each a mirror of the other. It absorbed the shock of their footfalls on the old steps.

However, nobody had yet figured out how to trod silently on the twelfth step down, which never failed to let out a weary groan. Word traveled around the student body that if a boy or girl wanted to sneak down to the kitchen for a forbidden midnight snack, the twelfth step on the right-hand staircase, and the second-to-last step on the left-hand flight of stairs must be avoided at all costs.

They all knew their headmistress possessed supersonic hearing; and furthermore, she never seemed to sleep—unless her house was on fire. *(You'll have to read about that in an earlier adventure.)*

Unfortunately, Father Lou wasn't a student at the school, and, overconfident in the carpet's ability to keep their secret, he allowed almost his full weight to fall on the accursed step number twelve.

All three of them froze at the protestation of the wood beneath the carpet.

"Whoever is coming down the steps had better have an outstanding reason," a haughty voice called out from the formal dining room. *(It was used mostly for grown-ups with more dollar bills than they could possibly spend without looking ridiculous.)* Sometimes Madrigal spread her work out on the shining maple table late at night. This happened to be one of those nights.

Father Lou raised a finger to his lips. Maybe she'd let it

go, assume she'd misheard, or believe that her sharp tone was enough to send the perpetrator running back upstairs.

Walter and Linus thought no such thing, feeling not at all surprised to hear the echoing sound of Madrigal's high heels clicking across the marble floor.

The sight of the three of them frozen like statues on her curved staircase actually stopped Madge in her tracks. "Lou?"

"Um, yeah. Hi, Maddie."

Maddie? thought Linus.

"And you two!" She pointed from Walter to Linus.

"Yes, ma'am," said Walter.

"Down here. Right now." Father Lou wasn't exempt from her accusing finger. "You too. Don't think you don't have any explaining to do, Lou."

They lined up in front of her.

"Do you know what time it is?"

Father Lou stepped forward. "Look, Maddie, I can explain."

"I'd like to hear it."

Walter opened his mouth. "I say, Miss—"

"Not you," she snapped. "Your yammering, even in that British accent, will not make things better for you tonight. Lou?"

Blast, thought Walter. Usually the accent worked wonders across the pond (in the United States), sometimes even with Madrigal Pierce.

"Ophelia is missing in the tunnels," Father Lou explained.

"With that boy Tom who's visiting Kyle," added Walter.

"What's happened to Tom?" a young voice asked from the balcony. There Kyle sat in his wheelchair next to the balustrade (railing).

Madrigal tapped her foot. "Back to bed, young man."

"But Tom's my friend. How long have they been gone?"

"About thirty minutes or so?" Father Lou asked Linus.

"Probably closer to forty-five by now," he answered. Linus tried his best to stay coolheaded; panicking would do no good. But all of this chitchat (light conversation) was beginning to collapse his foundation of calm.

"How did they manage to sneak past me?" Madrigal wanted to know.

"We found an entrance to the tunnels in the bookstore basement tonight," said Walter.

"And then the door locked behind them. We couldn't get through to go after them," said Father Lou.

"It was either come here or go to the cave entrance up river, and with the rain . . ."

"Hold it, Walter. You've been down there before tonight, haven't you? Did you get in through the school basement?"

"Maddie, please." Father Lou held up his hands. "There will be plenty of time later on for questioning Walter and Linus—"

"You too, Linus?" she asked

Thanks, Father Lou. Linus nodded.

"Maddie, time is of the essence. *Please.*"

Nobody could imagine telling her about Joe's presence.

"Let me change my clothes," she said, hurrying in the direction of her office.

"What? Why?" cried Father Lou.

"I know those tunnels like I know my own name, Father. I won't be long." She disappeared down the hallway.

"What are we going to do now?" asked Walter, running a hand through his curls.

"How are we going to explain Joe?" asked Linus.

"Just follow my lead, guys. We'll pretend we're just as surprised as she is," said Father Lou, walking toward the floorless parlor and looking down into the basement.

"And hope Tom and Ophelia catch on?" Linus asked.

"That's all I've got." Father Lou reached into his pocket for his flashlight.

"Will Tom and Ophelia be all right?" Kyle called down to them.

Linus ran up the stairs, not at all concerned with number twelve now. He knelt down by the boy's wheelchair. "They will. I promise, Kyle."

With that promise, the gravity of the present situation settled on him like a cape of iron ore, for he realized he couldn't make that promise. Not really. Not this time.

He rose to his feet.

"I'll stay right here," Kyle said.

"All right, man." Linus ruffled his hair and made it downstairs just as Madrigal emerged from the hallway, a pair of khaki work pants stuffed in dark green Wellington boots.

"Follow me," she said.

Linus garnered a great deal of comfort from her confidence.

sixteen

Unlikely Partners

or You Never Appreciate a Person until They're Under the Ground

Joe stepped silently behind them, his footfalls every bit as effective as Walter's. The only clue to his presence was a sudden intake of breath every so often. Ophelia surmised that, perhaps like herself, Joe felt these close quarters, and subterranean ones at that, more keenly at some moments than others.

Years later, as a student in the English Department at Kingscross University, Ophelia told me that her mind ran wild as she and Tom led Joe further down the main tunnel. She thought about the sheer weight of the stone overhead, the soil on top of that—now soaked with rain. Perhaps they were passing under a heavy brick house. And what if somehow, like Joe did later on in The Adventures of Tom Sawyer, *they became trapped—only to die of starvation? Wait, they would have no water source. That means they'd die of thirst well before they died of starvation.*

Small comfort.

Ophelia placed her hand around her throat and swallowed. And they had no water bottle this time.

By now Linus and Walter have surely realized that we're gone, she reasoned internally. *They're probably worried sick. They've probably followed us down here.*

The weight of that thought, picturing Joe's knife buried in her brother or her friend, was far greater than stones and dirt and even starvation.

Ophelia hadn't heard the latch click on the door as they were shut off from the rest of the world above ground. If it had been her, she would have gone for Father Lou's help. She hoped Linus exhibited the same good sense. She sent that thought flying from her brain, hoping that somehow her twin—the one she'd been with since the very moment her life began—would pick up the transmission.

Of course, you and I know that Linus possesses the same good sense that Ophelia does. And we also know that Linus can be very practical. But fear for a loved one's safety will cloud a person's mind sometimes, and certainly, more danger surrounded them all than ever before.

Linus, on the other hand, did not hold nearly as much mystery in his grasp as Ophelia did. He knew she was roaming the tunnels in the presence of a murderer.

Madrigal led them down the narrow tunnel from the school basement, a giant flashlight (more like a searchlight with a handle, according to Walter) lighting up the walls far better than anything they'd ever brought down there.

"Did anyone bring chalk?" asked Father Lou from his place at the back of their single-file line. His broad shoulders brushed the walls on either side of him.

Linus fished around in his hoodie pocket, his fingers sliding against the cool smoothness of the stick of chalk. "Got some."

"We won't need any," Madrigal called back. "I know these tunnels better than I know my own name."

"You've been down here quite a lot, then?" asked Walter, wondering why she repeated that phrase. He knew the importance of the Pierce name to the headmistress.

"You've met my brother," she said, her voice still crisply headmistress. "Would you rather be in a mansion with him or underground without him?"

"I see your point."

Johann Pierce would make anybody want to go subterranean. The man had set fire to the school in order to get the insurance money. Who wants to be around a person like that? He recalled Johann's hateful words to Madge on that fateful night of the fire: "You killed Mother on the day you were born."

"Besides," her voice softened now. "It's nice down here. Always cool, always quiet. I do my best thinking here."

Everyone left that alone. There was no sense trying to pry more information out of Madrigal Pierce than what she was willing to offer. It would be easier to tie a red blanket around your neck and fly like Superman.

They arrived at what Linus now thought of as the river tunnel.

"Let's head toward the cave," Madrigal said. "Hopefully they went that way."

"Should we split up?" asked Walter.

"There's strength in numbers," said Father Lou.

Madrigal stopped and turned, shining the flashlight down the line of males. Not knowing about Joe yet, she said, "Why should that matter? Both Walter and Linus have flashlights and chalk. The system is quite simple down that way. I think that's an excellent idea!"

Way to go, Father Lou, thought Linus. Normally having him along proved helpful. But tonight—sounding the alarm on the twelfth step, and now this—Linus began doubting his decision to bring the man along. He must have gotten soft in the head, being in love with Ronda and all. *Let's see how he gets us out of this one.*

"Wait." Walter raised his hand to shield his eyes against Madrigal's beam of light. "We found evidence earlier that the antiques burglar might be using these tunnels to store his or her loot."

"Are you sure?" Madrigal asked.

"Relatively so," said Linus.

"I wish you had said something earlier," she reprimanded them. "I would have brought my rope dart along." She turned back around.

Rope dart? Walter mouthed to the other two.

Right? mouthed Linus.

Father Lou wasn't surprised actually. Spend any time as a bounty hunter, and you'll soon learn that who people are and who they seem to be might not be one and the same.

Tom explored every side passage he could off the river tunnel. *He realizes*, Ophelia deduced, *that we're playing for time until the others find us.*

The first tunnel, if her judgment of how far they'd traveled was correct, ended at the basement of Ronda's hair salon. They met a brick wall there. Clearly an earlier resident of the narrow house on Rickshaw Street had located the tunnel and wanted nothing to do with it.

"What is this?" asked Joe. "I ain't never see'd a wall down here."

"You never knowed about any of this afore," said Tom.

"True enough."

"Let's get back to the main tunnel," suggested Ophelia.

Joe eyed her in the reflection of her flashlight. "Say. Why you wearin' them boy clothes?"

Tom sighed. "Do we tell him, Ophelia?"

"Tell me what?" Joe asked harshly. "You'd better tell me!"

"How did you get to that room you woke up in?" asked Ophelia.

"It was strange for certain," said Joe, as they continued on. "I got to the mouth of McDougal's Cave, and they'd put up an iron gate."

"Judge Thatcher did it," said Tom.

"That—" Joe spit instead of describing his feelings about Becky's upstanding father.

This is a fine example of the saying, "Actions speak louder than words." You can also apply that when someone who says they're your friend won't stand up for you when the other kids make fun of you. Ophelia could tell you about that sort of thing. Ask her about her classmate Sarah from sixth grade.

"What happened after that?" Tom called over his shoulder.

"Now, I ain't sure. I was sittin' thinkin' about how a body were to break through such doors, when this fancy feller come up behind me. I almost stabbed him."

"What did he do?" asked Ophelia, stalling for time. She knew how much people loved to talk about themselves. She also realized she might be able to gather some valuable information on traveling from Book World to Real World without the need for a circle.

"Said he knowed another way out. Then he did the

blamed oddest thing I ever see'd in my whole life. And I've see'd more'n my fair share."

Ophelia had no trouble believing that.

Joe stopped when they reached the river tunnel once again and leaned back against the wall, bending his right leg and resting his foot against the wall behind him.

By the way, Joe was dressed like any other person from St. Petersburg, Missouri, so you can stop picturing him in buckskin pants with fringe, moccasins, and a feather in his hair. If you don't like that, take it up with the author Samuel Clemens (Mark Twain's real name).

"He took a kind of stone out of his coat pocket. A soft stone. White. But not chalk. Then he drawed a circle 'round the both of us."

So a circle is still necessary! noted Ophelia.

Tom looked a little disappointed. Joe's journey seemed a whole lot more exciting than his had been. "What happened next?"

"He took out a jar of some kind of powder, sprinkled it just inside the lines of the circle. But that ain't even the strangest part. After the powder, he throwed a book down in front of us."

"What book?"

"How should I know? I caint read."

"Oh. Sorry," she said, briefly forgetting how many people were illiterate (unable to read) back then.

"Next thing I knowed, I was waking up in that room."

"Traveling usually makes people sleepy," Ophelia said.

"Traveling to where?" asked Joe.

"From McDougal's Cave to these here passages," said Tom.

"Then why're we lookin' for my treasure box if it ain't around here?" Joe pushed himself off the wall with his foot.

"We have to find our way back to McDougal's Cave first," said Ophelia.

"I reckon that's all we can do," Joe agreed.

Ophelia looked at her watch. 1:04 A.M. *How does time become so relative down here?* she wondered, wishing more than ever that Linus was with her. He'd know.

They set off once more down the river tunnel, another passage breaking off to their right. Tom took it. Ophelia tried gauging the distance once more, and as she did, she noticed the walls had changed to stone blocks, a heavily timbered ceiling holding up whatever rested on top. It reminded her of pictures she'd seen of old mineshafts. This was not a comfort.

"Look!" she cried as her flashlight lit up a table, some chairs, and other items arranged on pieces of furniture.

"Must be Birdwistell's tunnel!" Tom ran forward. "Look here, Ophelia. These chairs are just like the ones we saw on that box!" *(Of course, by "box" here, Tom meant Linus's computer.)*

"He *is* the burglar!" She rushed up to Tom. "I *knew* it!"

Sure enough, the two chairs were Louis the Fourteenth, and the sideboard was from Napoleon's time. She gasped. "Oh my!" Sitting on top of the sideboard was the Fabergé egg and an exquisite jewelry box.

"What's going on?" Joe caught up with them.

"Somebody's been stealin' fine things from folk in this town," said Tom. He reached forward and opened a drawer in a desk that hadn't been mentioned on any of the lists. "Look at this!" He pulled out a pendant hanging from a golden chain. "This one looks older'n any of this here stuff."

"Esmeralda's necklace!" Ophelia took the piece. "So Cato's in on this too!"

"Who's Cato? Who's Esmeralda?" Joe asked, his eyes glittering at the sight of the large emerald set in fine gold.

"Cato Grubbs is the fancy fellow who brought you here," she said.

Joe snatched the necklace from Ophelia's fingers. "This here'll fetch a pretty price in St. Louis." He slid the necklace into the pocket of his brown coat.

"Hey!" hollered Tom.

"It's okay." Ophelia held up a hand. "Let him keep it."

Joe's eyebrows raised in surprise, then lowered with suspicion.

"I know Esmeralda—the owner of that necklace," Ophelia explained. "Or rather, I know that she is not a nice person. She hurt a good friend of mine, and I don't like her."

Ophelia was referring to her friend Quasimodo, a sweet person whom Esmeralda had exploited (used for her own means without one bit of concern for his welfare) because he loved her and she knew he'd do anything for her.

Joe held up his knife again. "Now you shine that light on all o' this, and I'll just see what else I can find."

Ophelia hoped that Ronda had only somehow *misplaced* her jewelry and that it wasn't down here with the rest of Birdwistell's stash. When Joe stuffed the Fabergé egg into his pocket, she wanted to cry. "Oh!" she gasped, hoping that Real World objects stayed only for so long in Book World before they returned where they belong. Then she remembered what happened to the one ring to rule them all. She and Linus had gone back to their copy of *The Lord of the Rings* book and read the part where Frodo patted his pockets, looked all around him, and discovered the ring was nowhere to be found. He'd had no choice but to go back to Uncle Bilbo's house, settle down, and have lots of little Hobbits. With the ring gone, well, you can probably figure out what happened to all of those ugly, horrible, smelly orcs.

So much for the Fabergé egg.

When Cato returned to his secret room and found the trapdoor standing open and Joe missing, he laughed himself into such a coughing fit that he nearly passed out on his bed.

Two A.M. He was sure he had plenty of time to find Joe (after the man had made all the mischief he could, of course) and get him back to Book World before the acids ate him.

Once they were back in McDougal's Cave, Joe would lead him to the treasure. Cato had given the matter some thought. Even if he was, ultimately, stealing from Tom and Huck, he realized he simply didn't care about that. Why should they be set for life when everyone else had to work hard?

Well?

Madrigal filled them in on where each tunnel led. "That goes to the Randolphs'." A few minutes later. "That one goes to the house of the president of Kingscross University."

"Really?" asked Father Lou. "Why?"

"I don't know. It's a mystery why these tunnels even exist, Lou. If anybody could have found a clue, it would have been me."

Linus could believe that. The woman was more thorough than a tax accountant defending his client against the Internal Revenue Service. *(Ask your parents to explain; we've got more important matters to worry about right now, though many would beg to differ.)*

"Kingscross was founded four hundred years ago, wasn't it?" asked Walter. Four hundred years is no time for a Brit, but Walter knew it was positively ancient for an American.

"Yes, it was."

"What about smugglers?" Father Lou suggested.

"I've considered that, of course. But why the need for so many tunnels to so many houses?" Madrigal asked. "It seems to me that smugglers wouldn't need to go to such lengths."

True, thought Linus, peering ahead. According to his memory, they should be coming to the cave soon.

"What about a secret society, Maddie?" asked Father Lou. "Some kind of group that met for shady purposes unbeknownst to anybody else?"

She stopped again, shining her flashlight at the group. "Some kind of Mason-like group, only not the Masons?"

"I don't know. It just seems like people needed to leave their houses in secrecy."

"I think it's a brilliant idea," said Walter, hoping Madrigal would keep moving along. Every second Ophelia was missing delivered apprehension to his gut more faithfully than television anchors delivered bad news at six P.M. If they didn't find Ophelia and Tom soon, he'd start climbing the walls like Spider-Man.

"Sounds a bit fanciful for my taste." Madrigal dismissed the idea.

Linus whispered over his shoulder to Father Lou, "I like it."

"Thanks," he whispered back. "I appreciate the vote of confidence."

(Obviously, Linus didn't actually cast a vote just then. Father Lou just used the saying to express his gratitude that Linus deemed his explanation worthy of consideration.)

Three minutes later the river cave spread out in front of them.

Madrigal blew a puff of frustration from compressed lips. "I thought surely they'd end up here. It seemed a natural conclusion."

I don't know, thought Linus, *seems a bit fanciful for my taste.*

Walter felt like punching the cave wall. He kept his mouth shut. Better to say nothing than to spew the molten anger collecting in his chest.

Father Lou pointed to the empty set of shelves and the cot. "You boys think this is where the burglar is bringing the stolen items?"

"Yep," said Linus.

"He could get them out of the tunnels by using the river under the cover of night," surmised Walter.

Madrigal laughed. "Oh, that's funny!"

Walter knew it was wrong to hate someone, but right then he was coming as close to feeling hatred as he ever had before. Sometimes keen annoyance feels that way. He bit the inside of his lip.

"This is *my* territory," Madrigal explained. "I come down here every so often just to get away. Of course, now that you all know . . ."

"Your secret is safe with me, Maddie," Father Lou promised.

Walter sprung at the chance. She deserved it. "And if you forget about the fact that Linus, and Ophelia, and I came down here before, then it'll be safe with us, too."

"Lou, are these boys trying to strike a deal with me?"

Clearly no student had ever done the like. Walter was pleased.

"A good one," said Father Lou. "I'd take it if I were you."

"All right. No pots and pans."

Walter felt maybe .015 percent better. "Where to next, ma'am?"

"Back where we came from."

2:10 A.M.

How long is this going to take? Linus wondered. *Ophelia, I hope you're all right. Please be all right.*

seventeen

Sometimes the Road Less Traveled Is Less Traveled for a Reason

or Lead, Follow, or Get out of the Way

Madrigal stopped. "Wait just a second."

The males groaned.

She zipped to the edge of the cave and aimed her lamp at the river.

"What's wrong?" Father Lou gripped the back of his neck.

If a priest is annoyed, thought Walter, *then I must be all right.*

"The Bard is rising. After the last flood, I'm hoping the rain stops soon. We're at the highest point of the system here." She crossed the cave, returning to the group. "If the river rises even an inch above the floor here, the tunnels farther down will be almost completely under water." Her last few words trembled. "We'd better hurry."

At last! Walter shook his legs. "Let's go on, then."

Now Linus wasn't the type of person who prayed for every little thing. He figured he was given a good brain and a healthy body for a reason. But sometimes situations beyond the smartest brains or the strongest bodies made an appearance, and this was one of them.

He prayed the rain would stop.

If he had looked behind him, he would have seen Father Lou's lips moving soundlessly.

"We're lost, ain't we?" Joe grabbed Tom's arm as they came to yet another dead end, another stone wall, another basement. He jerked Tom around to face him.

"No! No, we ain't! The cave has got to be down one of these tunnels. Honest, Injun Joe!"

"Is he lyin'?" Joe shoved Tom away from him.

Ophelia caught Tom around the waist. "Truth is, we don't know where all of this leads. But we found that necklace, didn't we? Maybe others have stashed their stolen goods in here."

"We got to get back to them caves," said Joe. "I'll lead from now on. Well, sort of. You still have to lead us, but go where I say. I'm not taking any chances you'll run off behind me."

"But if you don't need us . . ." said Tom.

"You be quiet now!"

Joe pushed them back down the path toward the river tunnel. "Let's keep goin'."

They took a right again. Farther away from the school. Father away from the bookshop.

Ophelia noticed the path descending slightly. She remembered the river and the rain.

They walked for the next twenty minutes in silence. Why was Joe continuing? Surely he realized there was no finding that treasure by now.

Tom!

She thought about the murder of Doc Robinson, Joe's sense of revenge. Was Joe planning the same fate for Tom?

The tunnel curved a little to the left. A house tunnel snaked off to the right. The river tunnel had finally come to an end. Joe told them to go right, "Just to see," and twenty paces later they stood before another wooden door. Actually, there were two doors. The door in front was constructed of heavy iron bars such as one sees in neighborhoods where shopkeepers are more wary.

Ophelia reached out, grabbed a bar, and shook the door. "Locked tight."

"I reckon," said Tom. "Well, I guess we'll just have to go on back. Maybe McDougal's Cave is the other way."

Joe emitted a sound of disgust.

They walked back to the river tunnel's end. Ophelia shone her light on the end wall and the ceiling. Just like the tunnel by Birdwistell's, heavy beams held up the ceiling, the walls were constructed of rough stones.

"No," said Joe from behind, his voice low, dangerous. "We won't all be goin' back." He lunged at Tom as if this was what he'd been planning all along.

Soon after the makeshift search crew had exited the cave, Madrigal Pierce stopped once more. She shone her searchlight down a side tunnel. Linus noticed it was somewhat wider than the others.

"Let's try this one. It ends at the icehouse on the land belonging to the founder of the University. Nobody knows it's there, of course. It's how I usually get in."

Joe could have taken them anywhere, reasoned Linus. *While we're up this way, we should check it out.* He figured Walter, who looked calm enough, agreed.

Tom had been in fights before. He wasn't about to let Joe get the best of him, no sir. Some people possess a heightened sense of the importance of not only being alive, but also living that life to the fullest. Tom fell nicely into that category.

He stepped aside at the last moment, just as Ophelia tackled Joe from the side. The knife hit the floor and spun in Tom's direction. He grabbed it.

Ophelia yelled, "Run, Tom!" as she and Joe crashed together on the ground, her flashlight falling from her hand.

A rumbling sound startled them all. And before anyone realized what was going on, the tunnel ceiling began caving in. The roar attacked Ophelia's ears, and she turned her head, watching in horror as Tom, now twenty feet away, was separated from her by split timbers, rocks, dirt, and heavy, dried up roots.

Joe rolled her over roughly and leaned over her, one hand coming to rest on Ophelia's throat. The other hand joined the first, and they circled her narrow neck.

Ophelia couldn't scream.

Think! Think!

Ophelia wasn't a stranger to the odd fight when self-defense from a bully was necessary. She spread out her arm, reaching for anything. A crowbar would have been nice, but where's a crowbar when you need one?

Her fingers closed around a rock the size of a baseball, and four times as hard.

Joe started to squeeze. Ophelia felt her throat begin to flatten, and as she gagged and coughed, she swung her hand with as much force as she could muster, bashing the rock into the side of Joe's head.

A dull thud sounded. The weight of his body fell on top of Ophelia.

She coughed some more, trying to oust the squeezing sensation in her neck. She gathered her strength for several seconds (Joe was quite solid), arched her body with all her might, and rolled him off.

"Tom!" she cried, but she heard no response. Did the cave-in bury him? Oh no. Please, no!

"Ophelia!" Tom yelled, but he heard nothing in reply. He'd barely missed the rain of rock. Had Ophelia not been as lucky? Tom, now without a flashlight, hurried back toward the bookshop tunnel as quickly as he could in a darkness to which he hadn't yet become accustomed. How would he know the right tunnel? And why didn't he think to count them?

His anger at his own stupidity *(his words, according to Linus, not mine)* fueled him as he stumbled through the black corridor.

Ophelia scrambled to her feet.

Did I kill him?

She hoped not. Yet on the other hand, this was a dangerous person. He'd tried to kill her friend Tom! He'd just tried to kill her!

Ophelia realized then how much she had come to love that rascal from St. Petersburg. She'd always wanted a little brother, no offense to Linus, and Tom would have been a great one. A little lively, but so much the better.

She knelt down next to Joe and shone her flashlight on his face, then down his neck, settling the beam on his chest. It rose and fell with his shallow breaths.

She sat back on her heels, relief flooding through her. She didn't want to kill anybody. The knife was gone now, and hopefully once consciousness returned to him, a headache would follow—just for the fun of it.

In her pocket, her fingers found the measuring tape. Not taking any chances, she rolled Joe onto his stomach and reached for his wrist. Ophelia had gone through a macramé phase, and she knew a host of knots. Soon she'd bound his wrists so tightly together that even the Great Houdini (an illusionist and escapist during the turn of the century) would have had trouble working himself free.

Might as well start removing the debris, she thought. With the way she felt, alone and still afraid, that pile might as well have been Mount Everest.

Nevertheless, she reached for the first stone because that's what courageous people do.

You see, we tend to think of bravery as a single, heroic act of daring under trying circumstances, and certainly it can be just that. But sometimes courage is exhibited stone by stone and step by step until somehow the impossible is made probable, and the probable is made possible.

Tom couldn't have known it was almost 4:30 A.M. by the time he saw Madrigal's light at what seemed to be the end of the tunnel. But Walter certainly did. Linus had finally asked him to stop asking for the time. And when it was clear that Walter couldn't help himself, Linus peeled off his wristwatch and handed it to him. He knew Walter would announce the time when he deemed it necessary. And if the past two hours were any indication, it would be at fifteen-minute intervals.

The side trip to the icehouse proved as futile as the trek to the cave. The crew had almost made it back to the place of that poor first choice. Clearly, Ophelia, Tom, and Joe must have gone right at the river tunnel, not left.

One wrong turn, Linus thought with consternation. *Hang on, Ophelia!*

A sick feeling still coated his stomach, but so far the stabbing sensation that something terrible had happened to his twin remained at bay. Well, for a few minutes he felt extra sick, but then it passed. Surely, if Ophelia was gravely injured or worse (he pushed that possibility aside with all the inner strength he possessed), he would feel it, wouldn't he?

As they hurried down the river tunnel, he allowed himself to believe in the close connection he shared with his twin. They'd experienced it many times before. It wouldn't fail them now. He simply wouldn't allow it.

"Hey!" a small voice echoed from farther down the path.

"Who's there?" called Madrigal.

"It's Tom!" said Walter. "Are you all right?" he called back.

Tom caught up with the group. Alone. Linus felt his heart tumble inside his chest like a shoe in a dryer. "Where's Ophelia?" he asked.

Tom told the tale as succinctly (to the point, without extra words) as possible. When he got to the part about the cave-in, he panicked. He couldn't talk; his breath came in gasps.

Father Lou whacked his back. Tom sucked the dark air into his lungs and began to cough, then cry.

"Do you know if they're alive?" asked Madrigal, after she'd given him some water and he'd calmed down enough to finish telling the story.

"No, ma'am. There was a good twenty feet or so between us when the ceiling crashed down."

So she's either under the rubble or trapped behind it with

Joe. Linus allowed his fear to propel him forward. He grabbed Madrigal's flashlight and nobody tried to stop him.

I'd feel it if she were dead, he told himself over and over again. The mantra (repeated words) became perfectly timed with his footsteps, driving him forward into the narrow gloom.

eighteen

In Cahoots with the Enemy

or Another Secret Room—What a Surprise!

Linus hurried by the tunnel leading to the school. According to Walter it was now 4:45 A.M.

"Wait!" called Madrigal. "I'm going up to the surface. We need to get a rescue crew down here."

Linus, Walter, and Father Lou wondered how they were going to explain Joe, and even Tom, to the crew. And would the mysteries of the circle come to light? But just as quickly, thinking of Ophelia, they realized they didn't care.

"Good idea, Maddie," said Father Lou.

"And you're sure they're at the end of this very tunnel, Tom?" she asked.

"I reckon I'm positive, ma'am."

"All right. I'll see you all soon."

Madrigal disappeared down the narrow tunnel.

Linus continued forward, feeling calmer now, trusting that his sister was fine. The last Tom knew, Ophelia was alive. And she still was. She had to be.

Ophelia heard Joe stir before he even opened his eyes. She'd propped her flashlight on several large stones, trying her best to illuminate the rubble. She grabbed it now and focused it right on his face.

His lids opened, then lowered in a squint. "Get that lantern offa me, girl."

During the past two hours of digging, primal fury had soaked into Ophelia's cells. To say she was quite angry would be like saying Neil Armstrong was quite the little traveler. (*Neil Armstrong, in case your history teachers don't deserve their salaries, was the first man to walk on the moon.*)

"No!" she snapped. "You tried to kill me! I cannot believe you, Joe! First you try to stab Tom, then you try to strangle me. We're *children*! Is this the answer to all of your problems? Just kill people and everything will be fine? You know, I wanted to give you the benefit of the doubt, but now? You deserve to starve to death behind those iron gates!"

Joe, realizing that his hands were tied behind his back, struggled to get up. He pulled at the bonds.

"Don't bother," said Ophelia. "I'm excellent at tying knots."

He settled down. "What do you mean 'starve to death'?"

"You found those gates, didn't you?"

"I had just seen them when that fancy man brought me here, wherever *here* is."

"Nobody goes back to find you, Joe." She pulled her paperback book from her pocket. "It says it all here. They found you, your face close to the doors as if you were looking through that crack at the world you would never inhabit again. You tried to work your knife around the foundation beam, but of course it didn't work. There were bat bones, and you collected water, a few precious drops a day, from a stalactite. But it wasn't enough. I imagine it was horrifying. I imagine you had a lot of time to think about your life."

Joe's eyes grew round with horror.

"Nobody knew you were there because nobody cared," she finished. "And that—" she threw the book down "—is the sad story of your life. I hope you're happy."

I hate it when people say that, don't you?

Beyond them and unbeknownst to them, the amateur search crew had finally reached the location of the cave-in.

"Oh man," whispered Linus. "Ophelia!" he yelled as loudly as he could.

Father Lou and Walter did the same. Tom put his fingers in his mouth and blew out a piercing whistle.

"All at once," Father Lou said.

"Ophelia!" they shouted, the sum of their voices echoing back into their ears.

When the reverberating sound abated, a thick silence enveloped them. They barely breathed while listening for a reply, however faint. Thirty seconds passed. Forty.

"Let's start digging," said Linus. "What time is it, Walt?

"Almost 6 A.M."

They began digging, removing the rubble bit by tiny bit.

Linus hoped they wouldn't cause another shower of debris with their work, but what else could they do?

"And you know what else?" said Ophelia, not nearly finished. "After they found you, you became a hero. People came from seven miles away to attend your funeral. They buried you near the cave. You were pardoned by the governor of Missouri. People cried their eyes out, and some women were even appointed by committee to go into deep mourning for you."

Joe shook his head. "Stop. Please."

"Fine."

"I understand. Them people liked me a whole lot better when I was dead than when I was alive."

Ophelia hadn't even looked at it like that. "Well, yes. I suppose that's true."

"Maybe I could make it up to them somehow."

Ophelia snorted. "Yeah, right." She returned the flashlight to its stony cradle. "Besides. None of it matters if we don't dig ourselves out and get you back to the circle at our house."

"What happens if we don't?"

"Ever heard of the Wicked Witch of the West?" She knew, of course, that he hadn't, as *The Wonderful Wizard of Oz* had yet to be written back in Joe's time.

"No." Reason took over inside Joe's brain. "What is that book? And how does it know what happens to me?"

"You're going to have a hard time believing this," she said.

"I traveled through some kind of circle, girl. I could believe anything just about now."

She explained as she dug, realizing how silly it all sounded, but finished with great detail regarding what would happen if a character failed to make it back into the circle by 11:11 A.M.

"But I didn't come over like Tom did," said Joe.

"It doesn't matter." She picked up a stone and threw it over her shoulder toward the end of the tunnel. "Once a book is opened and closed, no matter who opened it, it's closed for good."

"Let me help you dig, then."

"No. You're too dangerous."

"You've given me good reason not to hurt you. Two work a whole lot faster 'n one. Please."

Ophelia brushed her hands together, dislodging some of the dirt. She crossed her arms. "All right. But you know the others are going to be digging for us on the other side, and if they cut through and find me dead, there's no way you're getting back to that attic."

"I hear you."

"Then let's dig."

Ophelia unfastened the measuring tape. And true to his word, Joe began digging and nothing more. He was strong and fast, and the pile of rubble abated (got smaller) that much quicker.

"Look here." Joe stood up, a rather large stone in his hands. "Git that light!"

Ophelia handed it to him.

He aimed it on a hole in the tunnel wall.

"Oh. Wow," said Ophelia.

The hole wasn't much bigger than the seat of a kitchen stool.

"Looks like there's a room in there." Joe shone the light through the opening. *(Ophelia had explained to him about batteries and electric power as best she could.)*

"We should check it out," said Ophelia. "I'm small enough to crawl through there, and there might be a way out."

She did just that, then reached a hand back out for the flashlight. Joe placed it in her palm. She shone it on the wall to her right. "Yep, this is definitely a room." Next, she shone the light on the wall facing her. "I see a door!"

She rose up, almost banging her head on the low ceiling.

She shuddered. The iron door resembled the large oven door in the witch's candy house from the story of Hansel and Gretel. "It's locked tight. There's no way we're getting out this way, unfortunately."

Ophelia turned back toward the spot where Joe was waiting for her, the flashlight beam illuminating the corner to the right of the hole. She screamed.

nineteen

Mystery Solved

or You'd Think They'd Be Able to, at Least Once, Get People Back to the Circle with Ten Minutes to Spare

The sound filled the chamber.

"Girl!" cried Joe. "What's goin' on?"

Stretched out in the beam of her flashlight sprawled a skeleton. In the corner where it had decomposed, its clothing was a collection of wrecked ribbons and rotted tatters.

Ophelia swallowed her fright. "A . . . a skeleton."

Joe stuck his head through the hole.

"And . . . I think I know whose it is."

Realizing that a pile of bones means no one any harm, and trying to summon up every bit of reason and pluck that life had bestowed upon her so far, Ophelia approached the now very deceased—judging by what seemed to be pants—man.

She dragged the light's beam from the bottom of his feet upward. Something glinted down inside his ribcage. "A dagger!" she said. "He was stabbed and then stuffed in here!"

"Maybe you'd better get outta there," said Joe.

Ophelia had to agree. She left the dagger where she found it. She was excited as she climbed out.

Joe noticed right away. "What is it?"

"A mystery solved! After a hundred years, we finally know what happened to Aloysius Pierce."

Hours passed as the Kingscross Rescue Team reinforced what remained of the ceiling overhead with fresh timber, while digging out the debris below. Both Linus and Walter wanted to help, but they also knew they would just get in the way.

"10 A.M." reported Walter.

Ophelia sat back on her heels. "I just can't do it anymore, Joe." She placed her hands in the light. Her fingertips were inflamed (swollen) and red; scrapes and cuts bloodied the backs of her hands.

"You just sit for a spell," Joe said, true kindness apparent in his tone for the first time.

"Thanks."

She sat on the tunnel floor, leaned back against the wall across from the hole where they'd found Aloysius's remains, and closed her eyes. It was already ten o'clock in the morning. She just couldn't imagine that they'd get Joe back to the circle in time. What would it be like to watch someone dissolve so painfully in the acids between the worlds? She had hoped never to find out.

At least it will be a quick passing, she thought. She *hoped*. What if they just stayed that way for all eternity? Stuck between the worlds? It was a horrible thought. No, that couldn't possibly be. Even Joe didn't deserve that.

"I been ponderin' somethin'," Joe said "If'n that fancy feller could come and take me afore I was dead in that cave, then could I return to another place as well? Supposin' we make it back to the circle in time."

"Oh yes!" said Ophelia. "That's the way it works. Why?"

Joe grabbed a stone. "I reckon I'd like to go back afore I killed Doc Robinson. I could do the diggin' job, take the money he give me, and leave town."

"That sounds like a fine plan to me. And you've got the necklace." Her voice dropped. "And that pretty egg."

He leaned back down to grab more rubble. "You like that egg, don't you?"

"Yes."

"It *is* pretty." Throwing more debris aside, he continued, "I don't want no fancy funeral or such only 'cause I starved to death. I'd rather have folks be sad 'cause I was a good man."

A pale face suddenly appeared at the hole in the wall, and Ophelia opened her mouth to scream again. But she'd used up all of her screams.

"You two should be in class," said Madrigal.

"Maddie, please," Father Lou said gently.

"Oh, I know. I'm just beside myself with worry, Lou."

Linus and Walter glanced at one another. Seeing this side of Madge was a good thing, but they both wished it could have been under better circumstances.

I've always found that circumstances precisely like the uncertain one down in that tunnel are where people reveal their most noble characteristics.

"It's 10:30," Walter whispered to Linus. "What about Tom? If we don't leave for the attic soon, I don't think we'll make it in time."

"I can't leave her, Walt."

"I know, mate. I can take him topside."

"What if you can't find the book? Last thing I knew, Ophelia had it in her pocket."

See what I mean about Linus's powers of observation?

"I suppose we'll just have to give it a go regardless." Walter wondered what else could possibly go wrong. "I'll go get him."

"For goodness sake, it's only me!" Cato Grubbs's head exited the hole completely. You couldn't say the same for his body.

Relief washed over Ophelia. "How did you—"

"This room is in the basement of the house where I kept Quasimodo."

A more foul dwelling I've yet to describe. If you must know what it is like, read about the trio's adventure with the hunchback of Notre Dame. I refuse to put myself through the trauma of creating a "sense of place" for that hovel more than once. If that bothers you, you'll simply have to make do and use your own imagination. I'm sure it's up to the task. Thank you. Please use the door marked exit.

Cato's secret comings and goings suddenly made sense to Ophelia. She once thought that he might have discovered some magic way to dematerialize and then show up again at another location. But how silly that was, she now realized. Cato was just as human as everyone else.

"How did you know we were here?" she asked.

"It's all over the news."

"But—"

"Never you mind, cousin. Why would I let you in on my secrets anyway? Anything I tell you won't be true."

"Well, *that's* true."

"All right, Joe. Let's get you back to where you came from. I need you to get me that treasure."

"How are you going to get him through that hole?" Ophelia asked.

"Never fear. I think of everything." He held up a vial. As he dropped a foul-smelling liquid, something akin to rotten eggs mixed with nuclear waste, on the stones of the wall below the hole, they began to melt away.

"Joe," whispered Ophelia, turning her back on Cato, her flashlight wedged under her armpit. "Here." She flipped the book open to the page where Joe, Muff Potter, and Doc Robinson are arguing in the graveyard. "Keep your thumb here and don't let him see that you've got it."

Cato finished his task. "Come on, Joe. Let's get out of here."

Ophelia wanted to hug Joe. Instead, she said, "Good-bye. And you can do it, Joe. You can be a good man. You *are* a good man. Just remember that."

"Oh please," drawled Cato. "Stop. I'm about to gag on all of that sticky sentiment filling the room."

Ophelia shone her light on the opening. Joe put one foot through, turned, stuffed something in her hand with a wink, and then he disappeared.

The egg.

Should she follow Cato and Joe? There could be another cave-in. But what if Walter and Linus found her gone? They'd think Joe was still with her, that she was in terrible danger.

The click of the iron door decided her fate.

Walter placed a hand on Tom's shoulder. "We've got to get back right away, Tom. And I'm not sure we'll make it back in time."

Tom didn't budge.

Ophelia's flashlight beam had been weakening for the last fifteen minutes. It faced the rubble, the circle of the beam narrowing its circumference until only blackness remained.

She shook it, clicked the switch on and off, and then rapped it against the palm of her hand with no success. The sum of exhaustion, thirst, and fear multiplied. She tried again with the same results.

That did it. It was dark. She was hungry, she had been up all night, she was all alone, and she was cold too.

She sat down on the tunnel floor and allowed herself a good cry.

"We're almost through!" said the captain of the rescue team.

"I hear her!" shouted Tom. "She's crying!"

"She's alive!" said Linus.

A team member pulled away a larger stone near the top, thereby removing the final barrier between the gang and Ophelia.

"Come on, mate." Walter pulled at Tom's arm. "Now!"

Tom jerked his arm from Walter's grasp and scrambled up the pile.

"Tom!" Father Lou cried. "What are you doing?"

"I ain't skeered!" he called over his shoulder. "Ophelia's afeard, and I aim to get to her!"

He slid headfirst on his belly over the apex of the pile, flowing like water over the top.

"Head's up!" a rescue worker yelled as more rocks and dirt fell onto the pile, closing Ophelia off once again.

When Ophelia heard Tom's voice, the tears went from your customary cats-and-dogs rainstorm to a typhoon.

Through her tears she could barely see him as he slid over the top, and the emergency lights behind the rubble only served to silhouette the boy.

And then, another cave-in?

She reached out in the darkness, her hands coming in contact with his soft hoodie. He put his arms around her and held her to him as tightly as his skinny arms would allow. Which was surprisingly tight.

"There, there, Ophelia. There, there." His voice was as calm as a baby asleep in her cradle.

So people really said that, Ophelia thought, finding his words more comforting than anything she had ever heard.

"There, there," Tom repeated. "Everything is gonna be all right."

She gulped down her tears. "Are you all right?"

"Just fine. They wanted me to get back to the circle, but I couldn't leave you here in the dark all by yourself."

"The time!" Ophelia's breath caught in her chest.

"About near circle time. But I'm not afraid, Ophelia. You'll be here with me. And I reckon that if I could see Becky Thatcher through, I can do the same for you."

Ophelia hated to play favorites; but Tom, well, he'd wormed his way into her heart like none of the others had. She hated to see him go more than she hated dangling modifiers—and that's saying something!

"I don't have the book with me anymore, Tom. I just don't know what's going to happen. I'm so sorry."

"You done . . . *did* . . .the best you knew how. I'll be all right. You just wait and see!" His courageous words shivered with a fear he tried to hide.

"I'm not scared," he whispered so quietly that Ophelia barely caught the words. "I'm not scared."

Walter checked Linus's watch. "Almost time, mate."

Father Lou hurried up to the boys. "They're through again. It shouldn't be long."

"It's 11:10, Father." Walter held up his wrist.

The priest closed his eyes. "Dear God."

"There's nothing we can do now," said Linus, feeling the sting of tears at the corners of his eyes. He cleared his throat.

"What's that light?" a rescue worker said as a green light spread its fingers through cracks at the top of the pile.

Walter began the countdown.

They all held their breath.

Ophelia and Tom affixed their gaze on the stone circle they'd hastily assembled just in case. The glow lit up both of their faces, shedding off one color of the spectrum for the next: green peeling off to blue, blue peeling away to reveal purple, then violet, red-orange, yellow, and finally that pure white light gently covered them like a motherly presence.

No sparklers shot up from the floor this time, however. The white light simply intensified, and Ophelia hugged Tom to her, cradling his head against her shoulder.

"Three . . . two . . . one," counted Walter.

They watched the changing light as voices of confusion erupted from the rescue crew.

The final white light shot through the rocks, swirled down among them, and then zipped off down the tunnel.

"What was that?" the captain said.

"I've never seen anything like it." Madrigal's eyes went from almonds to walnuts.

"It was . . . beautiful," said Father Lou.

Linus ran forward. "Ophelia! Can you hear me?"

"I'm all right!" her muffled voice sounded into the tunnel. "Tom's all right!" She began to laugh. "Tom's just fine!"

Ophelia felt Tom relax. He pulled his head away. "See? I told you everything would be just fine."

"And you were right!"

More stones were removed, and the work lights threw their beams against the walls. Ophelia could see Tom's face, streaked with tears. "You are the bravest person I've ever met, Tom Sawyer."

twenty

All's Well That Ends Well . . .
until the Next Time

or Tying Up Loose Ends—but Not All of Them, Mind You

Well, now I suppose you'll want to know what happened after all of that, won't you? Some writers prefer to end their stories so the reader will have to come up with the ending on their own. Heaven forbid if people live happily ever after anymore. Of course, happy endings aren't guaranteed in real life. Loved ones die. People are injured and are never quite the same afterward.

However! This is not one of those stories, I'm happy to report.

The gang emerged to the lights and microphones of news crews from miles around. The flashes from cameras blinded them a bit, and Madrigal spoke for them all, which was fine with Linus.

Poor Kyle was still waiting, twelve hours later, at the top of the stairs. The social studies teacher, Mr. Proctor, later explained to his boss, "We just couldn't convince him to budge."

"You did the best you could, Bob. Take the afternoon off. In fact—" she turned to the dirty, joyful group "—classes are canceled for the rest of the day!"

A great cheer erupted, and soon after Mr. Proctor ran into the cafeteria where the rest of the students were eating lunch, another cheer sounded.

"Maddie," said Father Lou, "I'm so proud of you."

"Well, thank you. And now I'm going to have a nice hot bath and put on some clean clothing. I suggest you all do the same. At seven o'clock tonight, we're going to have a party!"

Walter bumped Linus's shoulder with his own. "I could get used to this."

"You said it."

Ophelia drew up beside them. "We made it through."

Linus circled his arm around his sister's shoulder and drew her close to his side. "Miracles never cease."

"Look!" Ophelia pointed to the top of the staircase where Tom and Kyle were laughing together. "It's too bad he has to go back."

"Does he?" Walter raised an eyebrow.

Cato Grubbs crossed his arms, obviously trying not to slap them all, he was so angry. His red face coordinated nicely with his gold vest. "No treasure. Nothing underground but dead bodies."

"Which you were perfectly content to let us become," said Ophelia.

"He threw that blasted book down at the page you marked, and there we were at the graveyard. No treasure in sight," Cato complained.

Ophelia was having none of it. "We didn't bring him over. You did. You could have just gone in, found the treasure, and come back out."

Walter sighed, plopping down on the blue sofa. Push-ups could wait.

Tom entered the attic. "That shower is a wonderful thing."

Ophelia glanced at Cato, hoping he would follow Tom's lead. His ruffles were looking a little wilted and gray, and she wondered if she could get away with tucking a stick of deodorant in his pocket before he left.

"Why didn't Tom disintegrate?" asked Linus.

"You'd like to know that, wouldn't you?" If Cato had stuck out his tongue, he wouldn't have looked any less like a five year old.

"Have done, Grubbs," said Walter, the annoyance he felt in the tunnel not completely washed away.

Cato sat on Linus's stool. "Oh, all right then. It's nothing you can control anyway." He rested his elbows on the table behind him. "It's very simple. And it's so very sappy as to be embarrassing." He grimaced. "Sacrifice."

"Sacrifice?" Linus shook his head.

"Love, boy! Love! It's the strongest substance in the world, and it isn't even found on the periodic table of elements. Sickening, isn't it?"

Linus didn't get it. "Why should an emotion make any difference to a chemical reaction?"

Ophelia understood. "A cake baked with love tastes better."

"Precisely, cousin. It's why someday you will be much greater than even myself, Linus."

Oh brother, thought Ophelia.

"Your reasons for discovery will be more noble than my own." He arranged a ruffled cuff, his jeweled rings winking in the sunlight from the trefoil window.

"What about Tom?" asked Ophelia. "Not that we want you to leave," she assured the boy.

"The book is closed. I don't know how to get him back."

Ophelia grabbed Tom's hand.

"He wouldn't be the first one to stay," said Cato.

Linus couldn't believe what he was hearing.

Cato stood with a groan. "Ask Portia. Tell her about that wedding dress you found. Cheers, then."

Cato Grubbs, mad scientist at large, exited the room with a bow and a flourish of his hand.

"Tom?" Ophelia turned him to face her. "Are you okay?"

"From what you said, my life was over anyway, it bein' the end of the book and all. I'll just start a new one here. I reckon there's nothing else I can do."

"We'll help you, mate," Walter promised.

"We will," said Linus.

Ophelia hugged him once more. "See, Tom? It's like you said. Everything's going to be all right."

So there you have it, dear reader, another adventure come and gone. In case you were wondering, Birdwistell's house possessed no tunnel. The fact that his sister dealt in French antiques was entirely coincidental, which just goes to show you that jumping to conclusions never pays. The tunnel actually led to Jonas Clark's antique shop. And his sister Frances Clark-Sanderson attended various parties around Kingscross and scoped out possible antiques for removal. She was very good at finding and relieving people of their extra keys. Sometimes the truth makes the most sense. When Jonas Clark heard the news reports about the discovery of the loot down in the tunnel, he fled Kingscross with his dogs and took his sister with him. He's still at large to this day. Rumor has it they fled to Argentina.

Unfortunately, Birdwistell is still available to sniff in your presence any time.

Madrigal Pierce brought up Aloysius's bones and gave him a proper burial.

The emerald necklace Tom and Ophelia found belonged to Ronda, not Esmeralda. Yet Ophelia failed to utter a word about it, and Tom kept her secret.

The party at The Pierce School was, as the younger set says, a blast. And Walter made a good showing at the Kingscross 10K. Linus won the science fair and Ophelia's essay on the Pierce family came in second place, and then bumped up to first when the winner was found to have committed plagiarism (claiming another's words as one's own).

What about Tom and Aunt Portia? Well, you'll simply have to read the next book to find out. Talk about a hook!

Now, for heaven's sake, go outside. Ride your bike! Visit your best friend. Get that heart pumping and your blood moving. You can't sit around reading all day, can you?

THE END

Questions to Ponder

1. In the tunnels below Kingscross, Ophelia hoped to find a swimming pool, Walter hoped to find smuggled treasure. If you were to discover such a tunnel, what would you hope to find?

2. The three friends don't seem to like Professor Birdwistell and Madrigal Pierce too much. How did their opinions of these two adults change during the course of the story?

3. Ophelia can't stand the way Tom speaks, and at first she corrects him a lot. How does it feel to be corrected like that? Was she right to try to change him?

4. Will Linus ever figure out how the rainbow beaker works and what its purpose is? What do you think it does?

5. What are some of Tom's good qualities? What are some of Tom's bad qualities?

6. Would you want Tom Sawyer for a friend?

7. Bartholomew described Tom and Kyle's friendship as being like "kindred spirits." Do you have a friendship like that? How is it different than your other friendships?

8. Father Lou gave Tom a Bible even though he hadn't earned it. What did this teach Tom? What did it teach Ophelia?

9. The Easterday twins and Aunt Portia are keeping the enchanted circle a secret from Uncle Auggie. What will happen when he finds out?

10. Were you surprised to learn that Cato Grubbs uses the tunnel system and can't magically appear and disappear all over Kingscross? Were you disappointed?

11. If you could bring a fictional character through the circle and he or she never had to go back to Book World, who would you want to bring over and why?

12. What do you think Cato Grubbs was hinting at when he suggested that Ophelia ask Aunt Portia about that old wedding dress?

13. Bartholomew writes that "jumping to conclusions never pays." What does that mean? What conclusion did the four kids make about Professor Birdwistell? Did you believe he was guilty?

14. What surprised you about how Joe's behavior changed throughout the book? Do you think he deserves a chance to go back and get a different ending to his life story?

15. Linus hacked into Birdwistell's email account, Ophelia lied to Ms. Pierce about doing research for an essay contest, all three teens snuck into the tunnels more than once without permission, and then Walter made a bargain with Ms. Pierce so they wouldn't be punished for it. Does the end result (trying to find out who was stealing antiques) make it okay that they did these things?

The Enchanted Attic Book One

Facing the Hunchback of Notre Dame

Author: L.L. Samson

A hidden attic. A classic story. A very unexpected twist. Twin bookworms Ophelia and Linus Easterday discover a hidden attic that once belonged to a mad scientist. While relaxing in the attic and enjoying her latest book, *The Hunchback of Notre Dame*, Ophelia dozes off, and within moments finds herself facing a fully alive and completely bewildered Quasimodo. Ophelia and Linus team up with a clever neighbor, a hippy priest, and a college custodian, learning Quasimodo's story while searching for some way to get him back home—if he survives long enough in the Real World.

"A fantasy steeped in classic literature...narrator Bartholomew Inkster brings Lemony Snicket-like irony to frame the story....References to literature throughout the narrative make this a feast for middle-grade book lovers. Kids who like quirky adventure stories with idiosyncratic characters will enjoy a simpler kind of fun."

– Publishers Weekly

Softcover: 978-0-310-72795-8

Available in stores and online!

The Enchanted Attic Book Two

Saving Moby Dick

Author: L.L. Samson

This Character Could Be One Whale of a Problem

In Saving Moby Dick, Linus, Ophelia, and their friend Walter think they can control the powers of the Enchanted Attic, and they plan to bring Captain Ahab from Book World into Real World—on their own terms. But even the best-laid plans go awry sometimes, and their adventures take a wild turn. Captain Ahab is far crazier than they realized, and bookstores aren't really the best places to find whales, white or otherwise.

Available in stores and online!

The Enchanted Attic Book Three

Dueling with the Three Musketeers

Author: L.L. Samson

It all started with her Uncle's upcoming Chivalry and Romance and Loads of Frippery and Finery party...

Madrigal Pierce's greedy brother Johann has returned to The Pierce School For Young People. He owns half the mansion and plans to sell it. Fortunately, Ophelia has been reading The Three Musketeers, and Linus, Ophelia, and Walter decide D'Artagnan could rescue the school from his wily ways and keep their best friend Walter from going back to England. Their plan goes horribly awry—again—when the evil Lady DeWinter appears instead. Can D'Artagnan and the Three Musketeers save the day? Or is the school and the trio's friendship doomed!

"A fantasy steeped in classic literature...narrator Bartholomew Inkster brings Lemony Snicket-like irony to frame the story....References to literature throughout the narrative make this a feast for middle-grade book lovers. Kids who like quirky adventure stories with idiosyncratic characters will enjoy a simpler kind of fun."

– Publishers Weekly

Available in stores and online!

ZONDERVAN®
.com

Talk It Up!

Want free books?
First looks at the best new fiction?
Awesome exclusive merchandise?

We want to hear from you!

Give us your opinions on titles, covers, and stories.
Join the Z Street Team.

Email us at zstreetteam@zondervan.com
to sign up today!

Also—Friend us on Facebook!

www.facebook.com/goodteenreads

- Video Trailers
- Connect with your favorite authors
- Sneak peeks at new releases
- Giveaways
- Fun discussions
- And much more!